King Oberon's Forest

King Oberon's Forest

BY HILDA VAN STOCKUM

Illustrated by Brigid Marlin

New York

THE VIKING PRESS

LITHOGRAPHED IN THE U.S.A.

to

Martin and Moira Beausang

Contents

King Oberon's Forest

1. The Trick

It was King Oberon's favorite forest—everyone said so, especially the forest people. True, he spent much time abroad: there were battles to fight, dragons to conquer, feats to perform. But when he wanted to relax, he always went to this forest. There he had his palace, hidden in the center, and there he stayed whenever he could. Not that his people saw much of him; that was not to be expected. But it was comforting to know he was there.

He was a good king. To help an unfortunate subject he would not stop short of magic. There were few who did not praise him (nobody minded the old witch who lived in the elderberry tree; she grumbled at everything; not even the king was good enough for *her*).

The king loved the forest because it was a good forest. There was very little black magic in it. On the whole the animals and spirits got along well, though there were exceptions—there always are. And perhaps these exceptions worried the king. Who can tell?

The king also loved the forest because it was a beautiful forest. Nowhere else grew such a variety of trees, such thick moss, such picturesque shrubs. And it was, of course, at its best in the fall.

It was the last day of October, and Mr. Red Squirrel was taking his regular walk. He was at the age when one has to guard against getting fat. All around him the leaves were dropping gently, blending with moss and toadstools into a multicolored carpet. The summer birds had packed and left. Their empty nests hung like blots among the ever barer branches, and the woods were songless. Strong smells rose up from the earth—smells of leaves and fungi and ripening nuts, smells that set the other animals hurrying and scurrying to secure their winter provisions, smells that sent them digging and scratching, searching and stealing, burying and hiding, pulling and prying—but Mr. Red Squirrel merely sniffed the air and strolled about, admiring the scenery.

This is the finest autumn I've beheld yet, he thought. Aren't those bridal birches exquisite against the dark uniforms of the evergreens? Was there ever anything like the purple of that beech tree or the scarlet of that maple? But does anyone stop to admire it? No. Food, that's all the forest folk can think of. Food. No culture, no artistic sensibilities, anywhere.

Mr. Squirrel stroked his whiskers. He looked very handsome himself in a shaft of sunshine, which showed up the rich russet of his coat. Then he winced. He caught sight of a big oak tree, standing in an open space in the middle of the forest. This tree had the effect on him of an aching tooth. It belonged to three grumpy little dwarfs, and there was a long-standing feud between the dwarfs and the Squirrel family.

Not that Mr. Squirrel approved of feuds; he was against them entirely. As far as he was concerned, one person was as good as another, and the more the merrier. But tell that to the dwarfs! Stuffy little creatures. They *owned* their tree, and no one was to *touch* it. Wouldn't even let a fellow build a nest in it, though the air and location were much better there than in other parts of the forest. Called him a social climber, when he dared to mention it. Well, where would he be, without climbing? And social—of course he was social; but the dwarfs weren't, not they! Insulting, that's what they were. "Carrot tail," they had called him, though all his friends knew that his tail was auburn. And the references to the rest of his family had been so uncomplimentary that Mr. Squirrel had retired in dignified silence. At least, he hoped it had been dignified.

"Hey, Papa—"

Mr. Squirrel turned around. He saw his son, Ross, in an argument with a chipmunk.

"These are *our* nuts," Ross was saying. "I buried them here only yesterday."

"Finders, keepers," twittered the chipmunk, making off with as many as he could.

"Papa," cried Ross again, "please help me carry these nuts away! The chipmunks have discovered them. I know a place where we can hide them safely."

"Where?" asked Mr. Squirrel.

"Up in the dwarfs' tree," Ross told him.

"Are you joking?" asked his father. "Don't you know the dwarfs?"

"Everybody else knows them too," countered Ross with twinkling eyes.

"Ah, I see." Mr. Squirrel looked proudly at his son. "You think the nuts are less likely to be found there, eh?" And he thought he really must remember to tell Mamma about this. Ross was brighter than any of their other children; there was no doubt about it.

"They'll never give you permission, though," he objected. "You know what they think of us Squirrels."

"I'm not going to ask their permission," Ross answered cheerfully. "It won't be hard to sneak up that tree when they're not looking; they are usually in their little house, anyway, poking about. We'll hide our nuts in a hole I found in the top of the tree, and no one will come near it."

"You're *right*," said Mr. Squirrel. "Why didn't I think of it before!"

"You're too scared of those dwarfs," Ross told him. "They're just bluffers. What can they *do*?" Thus bolstering his father's courage, Ross led the way, with as many nuts as he could carry. His father, similarly loaded, followed.

One of the dwarfs was outside, raking the garden in front of his little house built in the trunk of the old oak tree. The squirrels could see his short, stocky figure dressed in blue overalls, a pointed black fur cap on his curly gray hair. His face was wrinkled like a walnut and ended in a short beard.

His task was difficult, as the leaves were not much smaller than himself. Frequently he would disappear underneath them, and only by wielding his little rake vigorously would he emerge again.

Mr. Squirrel, feeling rather silly, followed Ross to the back of the tree, out of sight of the dwarf, and climbed after his son to the hole at the top. They deposited their nuts and went for more. Back and forth they trotted. The hole was almost full when the dwarf discovered them.

"Mr. Squirrel!" he shouted in his most terrifying voice. (Unfortunately for him, it did not sound much louder than the chirping of a cricket.) "I thought we had made it clear that we do not *want* you in our tree. We can't have all the riffraff of the forest over our roof."

"Riffraff!" Mr. Squirrel snorted, deeply hurt, and dropped an acorn cup on the dwarf's hat.

"I'll have the law on you," squeaked the dwarf, waving his rake so wildly that he lost his balance and disappeared once more among the leaves. The squirrels laughed, and a passing rabbit, who had stopped to see what was going on, asked, "What's the matter?"

"It's just our usual quarrel with the dwarfs," Mr. Squirrel explained. "They won't have forest riffraff in their tree, they say."

"I like that!" cried the rabbit, who, though she had no desire to climb the oak, felt that she was included among the riffraff. "The *nerve* of them!"

"I think they are making a mistake when they say they own that tree," commented a wise old owl from a hemlock nearby. "They only had permission to build in it. It belongs to the forest. How would they like it if we owls claimed to own the trees we build our nests in?"

"Or if we said we owned the hill our hole is in," the rabbit added.

"We have to share *our* tree with others. Who do they think *they* are?" chirped a robin.

"Our father left us the tree in a deed!" cried the dwarf, whose head had emerged like a black truffle from under the gold and crimson of the leaves. "My brother has it locked up in a trunk. It's got red seals on it."

"Yes, locking up, that's what you're good at—locking up and sealing," chittered a few chipmunks. "Who else in the forest has keys and padlocks?"

Boos and whistles came from all directions, for a crowd was forming.

"Let them watch out tonight," cheeped a little mouse.

"Yes, tonight, tonight," echoed the other animals.

"Oh, misers, oh, hoarders, oh, grumblers,
Beware,
Tonight there's a magic, a spell in the
Air

"It's a feast for the gay and a farce
For the mean,
Beware all ye hoarders, tonight's
Halloween."

The dwarf looked comically dismayed when he heard this song. He thrust out his lower lip. "Don't you *dare* bother us tonight; don't you *dare!*" And he stamped his little foot on the ground with such fury that it actually made a noise.

"Come on, why don't you join us? We have lots of fun," chirped the robin.

"He wouldn't know what to do," Mr. Squirrel chided. "He can't play; he was born old."

"Three little brothers in a tree," sang the robin, "I don't like them and they don't like me."

"He-he-he," chorused the other animals.

"You are all very rude," the dwarf told them, drawing himself up to his full height, which was not particularly impressive. "Why don't you mind your own business?"

"Hoot, mon, you *are* our business. You're a blot on our landscape," the owl observed humorously.

"You're the bad spot in our tree," squeaked Ross.

The dwarf struggled with his indignation, which flashed in his eyes and bristled in his beard. "Wait till I tell my brothers on you," he threatened, throwing down his rake. Then he ran into his house, slamming the door so hard that all the branches of the oak tree quivered and acorns spattered around.

"Goodness, gracious, Brother Botolph," came a plaintive voice from the kitchen, where another dwarf was mopping the floor. "Please spare my nerves. You know how I suffer from headaches. Look what you did—all my pots and pans fell. And do you *have* to bring in all that trash?"

Brother Botolph looked down and saw that bits of moss and leaves still clung to his overalls. Some had spilled on the newly scrubbed floor. "Brother Alban," he cried, still full of his grievance, "come on out and tell those dreadful squirrels that this is *our* tree and that they've no business here. They are terribly rude; I can't get on with my work."

"That's your problem," Brother Alban answered. "I've my own. Look, you've made dirty footmarks too. As I feared, you got your feet wet again. Take these shoes off right away. Now you'll catch cold, of course, and keep us all awake with your coughing. I *do* think you might show some consideration for *me*. Brother Ubald, will you please get out of the way; I have to mop under your chair."

But Brother Ubald, the third dwarf, didn't budge. He sat hunched up on a chair with his nose in a book. He was very learned, and his thoughts were half a world away. Even shouting did not bring them back. So Brother Alban and Brother Botolph lifted him up, chair and all, and put him down somewhere else. He never even noticed it.

The three brothers had lived all their lives in the little house inside the oak tree. They kept very much to themselves, and were proud of it. They called it "minding their own business." They never visited, they never gossiped, they never borrowed, and they never lent. They each had their own work and went their own way.

Brother Ubald was the oldest, and he had the longest

beard. It almost reached to the tips of his pointed slippers. He had inherited his father's library, and as long as he could read undisturbed, he wished for nothing better.

Brother Botolph was the youngest and took care of the garden. It would have been pleasant work if it had not led to so many quarrels with the neighbors.

As for Brother Alban, he looked after the house, and his life was a misery to him. Whereas the others could each withdraw into their own, private sphere—Brother Botolph to the garden, and Brother Ubald to the library (which was built below the kitchen, between the roots of the tree, and could be reached by a winding staircase)—poor Brother Alban's domain was the kitchen, which also served as a living room. He therefore had to endure endless interruptions, and frequently declared that he could get nothing *done*.

His brothers tried not to annoy him, for he had a nasty temper. They did not smoke, because Brother Alban disapproved of ashes. They washed their hands often, because Brother Alban feared fingermarks. They went to bed early, because Brother Alban disliked candle grease. Even so, Brother Alban bemoaned their untidiness. And as for spiders, cockroaches, mosquitoes, ants, and the like, Brother Alban felt that hanging was too good for them.

At the present moment he was sulking because Brother Botolph had slammed the door. Brother Alban always suspected people of doing things on purpose. He was sure, now, that Brother Botolph had wanted to get even with him for accidentally stepping on his eggshell collection earlier in the day. Brother Botolph was very careless about his treasures. He left them lying about where a person couldn't see them. The eggshells weren't all broken, anyway. Such stupid things to collect, too—as if you could expect to keep eggshells forever! He couldn't understand why Brother Botolph had carried on so. Brother Alban kept defending himself in his own mind while he picked up the pots and pans and replaced them on their hooks.

There was a knock at the door, and with a sigh of a martyr Brother Alban opened it a few inches. "No!" he shouted. "I told you we don't give at the door. No, positively *not!*" And he shut it again quickly. "Those moths," he grumbled. "They think I have nothing else to do than to hunt up old socks for them to eat. Disgusting habit, anyway. Let them get their wool from the sheep—they've got plenty —instead of plaguing the life out of me."

Brother Botolph sat crouched on the floor, sadly fingering his remaining eggshells, which he kept in a cardboard box under the window sill. He thought Brother Alban *should* have known they were there. They were always there.

He had often begged leave to put them up on the mantelpiece, where they could be admired, but Brother Alban complained that they were too hard to dust. Brother Botolph now looked up with a frown and said bitterly, "What a fuss to make about a couple of moths. I wish you could see what

I suffer from those squirrels. *They* don't ask permission when *they* want to take anything."

"And how would you like to have bookworms biting off the endings to your best stories?" Brother Ubald demanded unexpectedly.

"Listen to the two of you!" cried Brother Alban. "You'd think you really had something to worry about, the way you talk. Actually both of you do just as you please. Brother Botolph goes on making his mud pies in the garden and collecting trash, and Brother Ubald spends his life dreaming. It is *I* who clean up your messes and do the work here, who make your beds and wash your clothes and cook your meals—"

"A fat lot you'd have to cook if *I* didn't make my 'mud pies' and grow the food for you," Brother Botolph retorted in a hurt tone.

"And a fat lot you know about studying," protested Brother Ubald. "I bet I could do your job with half the energy I expend on my so-called 'dreams.' Anyone can do menial labor. It is mental work that counts." And he stuck his nose in his book again.

"That's all the thanks *I* get," whimpered Brother Alban. "No one appreciates me. Oh, how my head aches!" And he sank to the floor, holding his forehead with one hand while he clutched a saucepan with the other.

"See what you've done?" Brother Botolph told Brother Ubald. "Now dinner will be late."

"I don't care, I don't want any dinner," Brother Ubald answered grumpily. "I ate too many onions yesterday."

"There was nothing wrong with the onions," snapped Brother Botolph.

"They disagreed with me," Brother Ubald insisted.

Brother Alban whimpered again. He looked around for sympathy, but his brothers didn't spare him a glance. At last he got tired of sitting on the cold floor and began to prepare dinner. "It's Halloween tonight too," he moaned, as if this were the last straw.

The three brothers disliked all parties, but Halloween seemed to them the worst. At Halloween it was the custom in the forest to give some of your newly gathered harvest to the creatures who knocked at your door. It was a way of taking care that even the crippled, incompetent, and lazy ones had enough to eat during the winter.

The dwarfs did not approve of this. "Why should shiftless people benefit by our labor?" they said. "It's only an excuse for merrymaking."

They had always refused to give anything. As a consequence, the forest children took a delight in playing tricks on them. They stuffed up their chimney, muddied their spotless windows, and trampled their garden. Once they had even got into the house and had made a terrible mess.

Therefore, when the sun had gone down in a red glow behind the dark trees, the dwarfs carefully fastened their shutters and locked their door.

"It's no use going to bed." Brother Alban sighed. "We won't sleep, anyway. We may as well light us a candle."

Outside, in the gloaming, creatures began to stir. A gust of wind brought with it a shred of eerie laughter. An owl hooted, and a mocking whisper rustled from tree to tree.

The three dwarfs sat gloomily around the kitchen table with its lone candle. They made a strange picture in the yellow light, which cast tall, flickering shadows on the circular wall behind them. They had the extraordinary habit of sitting with their backs to the table, letting the light shine from behind on whatever they were doing. They said it was less distracting that way, and that they saw one another's faces often enough.

Brother Ubald had his feet on the top rung of his chair. His knees were humped up, supporting a large book, which hid his ears.

Brother Botolph's back was bowed over a seed catalogue, and Brother Alban held a slate on his crossed legs. He was trying to do his household accounts.

The grandfather clock ticked slowly. The kettle sang a plaintive song on the stove. Brother Alban's pencil squeaked.

"Oh, do stop that noise," grumbled Brother Botolph. "That's the second time I've lost my place."

"I've got to add," complained Brother Alban. "Two jars of preserved mushrooms and three jars of preserved beans and twelve jars of gooseberry jam makes seventeen jars— squeeeak—"

Brother Ubald winced and pulled his book closer about his ears. There was a sound of trampling feet outside and a loud knocking at the door. A hoarse voice cried, "Tricks or treats!"

The three brothers clenched their fists and remained silent. The door stayed shut.

"Perhaps they'll think we're out," whispered Brother Botolph.

"Not a hope," Brother Alban whispered back.

There was a moment's hush outside; then the knocking at

the door started again. "Tricks or treats," squeaked a high voice.

"Go away," Brother Alban growled.

There was another silence, which made the dwarfs hope that the visitors had left. But then the house began to rock on its roots. Several pictures fell from the walls, and all the pots and pans came clattering down on the kitchen floor again.

"Somebody must be shaking the tree, somebody *big*." The dwarfs blanched with fright.

There was more knocking at the door, while a ghostly voice sighed, "Tricks or treeeats . . ."

Brother Botolph's nerves snapped. "Tricks!" he shouted.

"Eeeeeeeeeeeh!" squealed a chorus outside. Then there was another silence, while the three dwarfs looked anxiously at one another. Would the house be uprooted this time?

"Serve them right, the old skinflints," came the voice of a badger, followed by the tittering of sparrows.

"They'll have their hands full with this trick," croaked a raven.

"No more lazy days for them," squeaked a chipmunk. "Let's wait and see what they'll do."

"It will be the wrong thing for sure." They heard more laughter, and then silence.

The three dwarfs trembled. Some evil had been done to them, and they couldn't guess what.

"They may have painted a skeleton on our door," whispered Brother Alban.

"Or they've set fire to the tree—"

"Or they've flooded my garden. I've got to go and see," worried Brother Botolph. He took a lantern from the shelf and lit it.

"Don't, on any account, open the door," warned Brother Alban.

But Brother Botolph had already done so, letting a stream of fresh air into the close room with its smell of candle grease. There was a screech from the animals outside, who had gathered on the dwarfs' front lawn and now scampered off to hide. Only their glowing eyes were visible here and there among the trees.

Brother Botolph held up his lantern and peered into the darkness. A thin thread of sound at his feet made him look down. Rolled up in a cabbage leaf, like a small sausage, lay something that moved and cried. Brother Botolph put down his lantern and examined it. It was a newborn baby of some kind or another—a little too frail for a young dwarf, not furry enough to be an animal, and too plump to be an insect. He noticed that there was a piece of paper tied to the cabbage leaf, and he was startled to see that it bore the gold seal of King Oberon. Holding it in the lantern light, he read what was written on it.

" 'Inasmuch as this baby is left an orphan by the untimely deaths of his parents, the king hereby wishes it to be brought

up by his forest, and recommends it to the mercy of his people. Signed, on this thirty-first day of October, by Prince Sylvester, secretary to King Oberon.' "

Brother Botolph heard a suppressed tittering behind the trees. He cried angrily, "What is this? Why is this infant not looked after? The king has said that the forest is to take care of it. Why is it lying here?"

There were more titters, and a shrill voice cried, "It's yours; it's a present."

Brother Botolph stamped his foot. He picked up the baby and held it out. "Don't trifle with the king's order. Bring the child to the orphanage immediately, before it catches cold."

"The orphanage is full," hooted an owl. "Nor have you ever supported it or given alms to anyone in the forest. It is now your turn. It's up to *you*."

"*Me? I'm* to look after it? Nonsense!" cried the dwarf. "Surely there is a mother among you who can do it better?"

"I've got six of my own," came the voice of an indignant rabbit.

"We've to work for our living," snapped a chipmunk.

"Too poor—" wailed a rat.

"And so you saddle *us* with him," growled Brother Botolph. "I'll protest to the king. We're three bachelors; we can't—"

"The forest has decided that you can . . . you can . . . you can . . . ," sang the voices, which sounded fainter and fainter, until they faded entirely. There was a rustle and a sigh, and then silence.

Brother Botolph stood alone in the starlight, holding his lantern with one hand and a squirming baby with the other. He stood and stared until Brother Alban pulled him inside, closing the door behind him.

"What's the matter, Brother Botolph?" he asked anxiously. "Did they put a spell on you?"

"No, look—it's this." And Brother Botolph showed his burden.

"Don't touch it! It's a trick! Throw it into the fire!" cried Brother Alban.

"It may be a trick, but it's also a baby." Brother Botolph sighed. "As a matter of fact, it's an orphan whom the king has entrusted to us."

"Good heavens," exclaimed Brother Ubald, putting on his glasses and examining the infant, "you'd better be careful! It's a fairy-nestling of the variety of *Felix hilaris spiritus*. Look at its dragonfly wings! Don't, I beg of you, hurt a hair on its head, or you'll bring all of Fairyland down on us, not to mention the king."

"Well, why don't they take care of their own, then?" grumbled Brother Alban. "Have they no orphanages? It would be far too much trouble for *me* to look after. I'm not getting any younger. It would mean more clothes to wash, more food to prepare, more mending to do. But, of course, that does not matter. I work and slave and nobody cares."

He stopped, hoping to hear his brothers protest that they *did* care, and that they had no intention of allowing him to be thus burdened.

Instead, they were tickling the baby.

"All right, melt over him, keep him if you like, but we'll never have a moment's peace again, and don't say I didn't warn you. Before this the noise was at least *outside* the house; now it's inside. Listen to him squalling!"

"That may be because Brother Botolph is holding him upside down," Brother Ubald pointed out sagely. "I believe sideways would be better."

"Tulips are held this way," Brother Botolph defended himself. But he did as Brother Ubald had suggested, and, indeed, the baby stopped crying. It lay perfectly still for a moment and then it gave an enchanting smile.

"The creature . . ." murmured Brother Botolph, looking at it with the tenderness he usually reserved for his eggshells. "Won't it be fun to see him grow?"

"And *how* will he grow?" asked Brother Alban. "Do *you* know how to take care of a baby?"

That was, indeed, the difficulty. None of the dwarfs had any idea. It had been too long since they had been babies themselves. But Brother Ubald went to his library and consulted a book called *Fairies and How They Grow. Scientific Observations Made at King Oberon's Nurseries by Andrew McTavish, Court Physician.* He came back with his finger in a passage, which read, "Keep fairy babies in a warm, dry bed; feed them a spoonful of honey every hour; and soothe them with melodious tunes."

Brother Alban grumpily fetched a laundry basket, in which he placed a folded blanket. This made a warm, dry bed. Then Brother Botolph extracted some honey from potted plants and fed it to the baby. Now came the most difficult part: the melodious tunes. They hadn't a phonograph, or piano, or even a canary.

Later that night several mischievous spirits, returning from their revelries, felt curious to see what the dwarfs were doing with their foundling. So they went to the oak-tree house and peeped through the hole in the shutters.

What they saw amused them greatly.

The three brothers were gathered around the improvised cradle, singing with all their might. Brother Ubald's voice squeaked on the high notes, and Brother Alban's croaked on the low ones, while Brother Botolph's was scratchy all over.

But the baby was fast asleep.

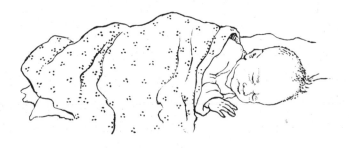

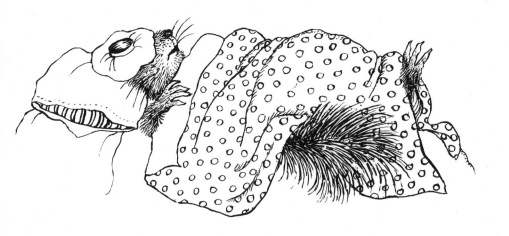

2. Troubles

The next morning, when the first gray mists still floated between dreaming trees, there were groans from many nests and holes as the forest children awoke.

"Oh my head!" said Mr. Red Squirrel. "Mamma, bring me some coffee." When she had gone, he asked, "Ross, what did we do last night?"

"I can't remember," said Ross. "Except that you were dancing all the time with Miss Rosie Chipmunk."

"Oooooooh," groaned his father, pulling his blanket over his ears. "Don't tell Mamma, or we'll never hear the end of it. What else did we do?"

"You drank too much elderberry wine and sang the song Mamma doesn't like," Ross went on, with a certain pleasure in his father's confusion.

"Don't tell her," his father pleaded hurriedly.

"Will you let me go off, then, on that hike with Jimmy Woodchuck?" asked Ross.

"Sure, sure," said his father. "Oooooooh, my head. You are certain that is all we did?"

"You did, you mean," said Ross priggishly. *"I* didn't do anything, except peer through the windows at the dwarfs."

"Oh, and what did you see?" asked Mr. Squirrel.

"I saw them sing," said Ross, with a grin. "Oh Papa, you missed something."

"Hm," mused his father. "It's all very well for the first night, but I wonder how they are going to manage."

That was what the dwarfs were wondering too, as they looked down on the fairy infant and realized that he wasn't a dream after all.

"We must get rid of him," decided Brother Alban. "It's preposterous."

The other two didn't answer. They gazed at the baby, and into their old faces stole an expression that could have been a smile if their wrinkles hadn't pointed the other way.

"We must get rid of him as soon as we find a good home for him," Brother Alban repeated, and he began to polish furniture industriously.

It was all very well, he muttered to himself, babies were delightful, sweet, and all that; helpless too; in need of care —true. But what did it all amount to except trouble—

trouble for Brother Alban? So he refused to be charmed, and treated the infant as an unwelcome and temporary guest.

Surprisingly, the little creature showed a decided preference for Brother Alban: it favored no one else with such smiles and gurgles and outstretched arms; and though Brother Alban's stern face did not relax, he did admit that the baby was no fool. But then he immediately pointed out how right he had been in his prediction that peace would fly with the baby's arrival. For one thing there was constant knocking at the door. Those impudent squirrels who had trespassed on their oak tree had come to ask after the baby, and a Mrs. Mole they'd never even *heard* of wanted to know if they'd like to borrow her baby buggy. Then there was a Mrs. Powderpuff, cousin to Jack Rabbit, who had the effrontery to offer them a bowl of soup—as if Brother Alban weren't capable of making his own! These were all pretexts, of course, to satisfy their curiosity and gloat over the dwarfs' trouble. Well, the dwarfs sent them about their business with ringing words, and slammed the door after them—good riddance!

But they could not enjoy their peace, for they found the baby tossing about and wailing with a high fever. You could feel it right through the blanket.

"He has caught a cold; the door has been open too many times," said Brother Alban.

"Nothing of the sort," contradicted Brother Ubald, who

had consulted his book on fairy babies. "It's the noise. We've been shouting and slamming the door. That gives fairy babies a fever."

It was quite extraordinary how softly the dwarfs moved after that, and how gently they reproached one another. The baby recovered immediately, to their great joy.

Brother Alban didn't mention getting rid of him again. He treated him now with the same consideration he showed his pots and pans. He even called him by his fairy name, Felix hilaris spiritus, which was soon shortened to just Felix. The baby was enough trouble without adding a long name.

The dwarfs wondered how such a small creature could make such a big difference to their lives—but he did. For one thing, he was the only responsibility they held in common, and this led to a lot of friction (though they didn't dare shout any more).

It was Brother Botolph's job to feed Felix, but one day when he was planting some particularly valuable bulbs, he forgot. The baby made such a commotion that Brother Ubald and Brother Alban thought he was going to die of convulsions. Brother Alban didn't get the dishes washed that day, and Brother Ubald held his books upside down and never even noticed. Both dwarfs were furious with Brother Botolph, and made him carry an alarm clock in his pocket so he would not forget again. Brother Botolph complained that the heavy clock got in his way and tore off his pockets and scared him out of his wits every time it went off; but his brothers told him it was just too bad, he'd have to bear it.

"Why doesn't Brother Alban feed the baby? He is in the kitchen, and it would be much easier for him," Brother Botolph protested.

This made Brother Alban very angry. "Who brought the baby into this house in the first place?" he hissed (very softly). "And who is always playing with him and tickling him and calling him 'sugar-plum' and 'honeybunch'? So you want all the fun and none of the work, eh? You'd better do your share, or I'll give him to the first witch that passes the house."

"Oh, all right, all right," grumbled Brother Botolph, re-signedly cramming the alarm clock back in his pocket. But he hated the thing. He jumped like a grasshopper every time it went off, and he dreamed of it at night. He often thought wistfully of the lovely days when his only worry was a silly little quarrel with the neighbors.

And then, suddenly, the baby developed spots all over his body—red, green, and purple spots. The dwarfs couldn't imagine what it meant. They thought of measles, but measles spots were always uniformly red.

Brother Ubald had to take out his book again, and he discovered that fairy babies develop a multicolored rash when they have not been bathed enough.

"Did you know babies should be bathed?" asked Brother Ubald.

"I wanted to bathe him all the time," confessed Brother Alban. "Only he seemed too fragile."

"Well, it says here we've *got* to bathe him," Brother Ubald observed, a big frown on his forehead. "I think I shall attempt to do so. It is an important job, Brother Alban. Leave this to me."

Brother Ubald was never one to undertake things lightly. First he studied three big books. One was called *Ablutions and Their Effect on the Nature and Temperament of Fairies* by Professor Bulldog. The other was called *How to Wash Well in Ten Easy Lessons* by Miss Tabby Cat; and the third had the significant title, *The Dangers of Too Much Water on the Respiratory System* by Lady Toad-Tadpole.

"I think I understand the principle now," he remarked, shutting the last volume. "The main thing is to keep the pores open and the mouth closed." He looked around. "Now we shall have to get the accessories. Where is a bath?"

Brother Alban brought him a dishpan and some towels. Then he brought him a cake of soap and the baby—all this while Brother Ubald sat on a chair and meditated. "What do I do now?" he asked, receiving the baby on his lap.

"You undress him," said Brother Alban.

"Oh."

It was a wondrous sight to behold Brother Ubald undressing the baby. His scholarly face bent attentively over the squirming bundle on his lap, much as if it were an unread manuscript. His unaccustomed fingers fumbled with the

knots and buttons, and his slow, learned movements were no match for the infant's quick defenses. The two were soon at cross purposes, and a regular battle ensued, which terminated in a tearing sound as Brother Ubald forced apart Felix and his clothes. Luckily it was the dress that was torn, not Felix, but the child cried as loudly as if it had been the other way around.

Now that the baby was naked he was twice as hard to handle. Brother Ubald had a book propped up beside him from which he read instructions. Unfortunately his attention was so much on the book that he didn't notice how the soaped-up baby slithered from his grasp and disappeared under water. He found out just in time and retrieved the child by his two feet, the only part of his body that was still visible. But Felix's lungs were so full of water that he could not breathe. He just sat there with a purpling face till Brother Alban saw him, grabbed him, and smacked the water out of him. Then he heaved a long breath and paled down.

"You see," said Brother Alban. "That's what I was afraid of. You and your books!"

Brother Ubald frowned. "I suppose I shall have to learn the instructions by heart," he concluded. "And do I have to put all his clothes on again now? I just took them off."

"Yes, and tore the dress past mending," Brother Alban commented. "Never mind; here is a clean one."

Brother Ubald sighed. "Bathing a baby is very hard," he complained. "Do I have to do it every day?"

Brother Botolph had entered the kitchen. "Here," he said to Brother Ubald. "You take the alarm clock, and I'll do the bathing."

Brother Ubald thought this a good exchange. It would be no trouble to feed the baby honey every hour or so. He liked to hold the little thing and watch the tiny hand curl around the spoon while the little legs crossed themselves in the air and the dark eyes opened and closed with rapture.

Brother Botolph had a wonderful solution to the bath problem. He simply sat the baby in the sink and poured warm water on him from his watering can. Felix liked it, and Brother Alban didn't mind as long as Brother Botolph wiped up the stray drops.

But Brother Ubald's quiet reading days were over. At first he didn't hear the alarm clock at all. Then he began to wait for its shrill tinkle and could not keep his mind on his books. It was difficult not to spill honey when the baby moved his head, and sometimes the honey went in too fast, or the baby swallowed air. Then he would cry until Brother Ubald paced the floor with him, the downy head held against his ear as he patted up fairy bubbles. Even when he slept Brother Ubald would take fright suddenly and put down his book to see if perhaps the baby had been smothered in his blanket.

At night the three dwarfs would sit around the kitchen table, stroke their tired foreheads, and complain.

"Nothing is tidy any more; everyone thinks he can borrow my things and bump into me. Brother Ubald, you messed honey on the floor again, and I knocked my shins blue against Brother Botolph's watering can," Brother Alban would lament.

"And *my* life, then—" Brother Ubald groaned. "I don't remember anything I've read, I'm growing duller every day, all my books are sticky, and no one mends the holes in my socks."

"What about *me*?" Brother Botolph countered. "I am the one who wakes up at night and takes care Felix is covered and hasn't a tummy ache. You both snore through everything. It all comes from dreaming of that alarm clock; it wakes me every hour of the night. In the daytime I'm so tired I fall asleep over my eggshells. Oh, for the good old days!"

It was midwinter now, and the forest was hushed with snow. The trees stood glittering in their armor of ice. Now and again a twig would crackle and snap and ice would tinkle down.

Animals stayed in their holes and slept as much as possible, except when hunger drove them to walk over the snow, leaving their footsteps behind like a string of beads.

Mamma squirrel was a good housekeeper and kept her family warm and comfortable. She relied a lot on Ross, who was a dependable youngster and a good deal more help than Scarlet and Pinkie, his empty-headed sisters.

"Our supplies are getting low, Ross," she remarked one evening as she put the last acorns into the soup. "I wonder, would you run out and see if we have some more hidden somewhere? Your pa is, of course, nowhere to be seen." And Mamma Squirrel sighed. Pa had been a romantic character whom it had been exciting to marry, but the trouble was that he had stayed romantic. Domestic affairs bored him.

"Sure, Ma, we still have the nuts in the dwarfs' tree; we kept them for last, as they were safest. I'll go right away," said the good Ross, pinching his sisters as he went out.

The snow was violet-blue against the dark brown of the oak tree. The orange squares of the lighted windows threw yellow patches on the snow. Ross knew that the dwarfs were not in the habit of burning light. He wondered what had happened. As he passed with his nuts he peeked inside.

The old dwarf with the long beard was walking up and down with the baby, who was yelling. Another dwarf was bringing a hot-water bottle. The third one was waving a homemade rattle. All three were obviously exhausted. Drops stood on their foreheads.

Ross chuckled. "Trouble, eh?" he said to himself. "Serves them right, the meanies."

He recounted what he had seen at home, where Mamma was ladling out the soup.

"Poor thing," she said. "Scarlet, will you please *not* put your tail in the soup! I don't care if it's hot; it isn't manners. And, Pinkie, the table is no place to trim your nails. Look at Ross, he knows how to behave. . . . What was it you said, son? Oh yes, that poor baby. I always thought it was a cruel trick to play on a child—I would have taken him myself if Pinkie hadn't come down with the mumps just at that moment. . . . Finish your plate, dear; there's lots of little creatures starving in the wood this minute, so you should be grateful for your food. As I was saying, that poor baby, with those dreadful old dwarfs—"

"Poor dwarfs, I say," grumbled Mr. Squirrel, who was out of humor with the world. He had the itch in his legs, and when he had the itch in his legs he wanted to wander far, far away and liberate a captive princess. But his wife kept her eye on him, and he knew he hadn't a chance.

"Poor dwarfs, they were living their own lives, happy and independent, and we have to saddle them with a baby. Ugh!"

The following weeks, as they went back and forth for nuts, the squirrels reported home what they had seen through the windows in the oak tree.

"The baby is growing," said Mr. Squirrel. "He's sitting up in a chair now. I don't think he's a bit unhappy."

"Poor child," was all Mamma Squirrel said to that.

One day both Ross and her husband came back from their expedition, twinkling with merriment.

"Listen to what happened—" began Ross.

"You hush up and let your father talk," Mr. Squirrel told him. "We saw a most amusing thing. The fairy child said 'Papa' today to one of the dwarfs. You should have seen how tickled he was; he grew pink from the beard up. The other dwarfs were jealous, of course."

"Yes," Ross chipped in. "They kept asking him to say 'Papa' to *them,* but he wouldn't, and he pulled the old one with the long beard by the nose. Oh, I had to laugh."

"I must go and look some time," said Mamma, "when it's a little warmer."

There were others who peeked through the windows— the dwarfs often had an audience, but they were so busy with the baby that they never suspected it.

3. Growth

As Felix grew, so did trouble grow with him. Before the winter was out, he was walking. Then the dwarfs realized what an easy time they had had while he was still lying in his clothes basket.

Now he was all over the place—you'd scarcely hear his merry little voice in one corner than you'd see him in another. He climbed all over Brother Ubald's books, getting himself black with dust, and then he'd fall asleep on Brother Alban's newly washed and ironed linen. He awoke early in the morning, singing with the sparrows (a lovely little voice he had, too), and if the dwarfs didn't get up right away to make him some pollen porridge he'd climb on their beds and tickle their noses till they sneezed. If one of the dwarfs pulled an angry face, Felix would look this way, and then

45

that way, and peer through his fingers. Finally he would stand on his head and look at the dwarf from below. When the dwarf couldn't help smiling, Felix would clap his hands.

But it wasn't only the walking that was troublesome; the talking became almost worse.

First it was "What? What? What?" all the time. Brother Alban and Brother Botolph answered his questions— "That's a spoon there. . . . That's a knife, don't touch. . . . That's fire. . . . That's water. . . . That's a flower." But when Felix asked, "Who made me?" Brother Alban referred him to Brother Ubald. He remembered that long, long ago his mother had told him something of that nature, but he wouldn't know how it went any more. Brother Ubald took a dusty fairy Bible from the shelf and found the answer.

"The great Pan made you."

"Who is Pan?"

"He is the god of Fairyland."

"And where is he? When can I see him?"

"You are seeing him."

"No, I'm not."

"Yes, you are—you see me, and this room, and the sky and the trees. Everything is in Pan, and Pan is in every-thing."

"But I want to see him the way he *is.*"

"No, we can't see him that way because he hasn't a body —he is a spirit. The person most like him, here in the forest, is King Oberon."

"I want to see the king."

"Well, perhaps someday you will."

"Why did Pan create me?"

"Because he loves making things. He is at it all the time, especially in the spring. Right now it is winter, and he is taking a bit of a rest."

"Can I make things too?"

"Yes, you may make a paper boat. I'll teach you how."

And so Felix was put to work, which stopped the questions for a while, but not for long. Before Brother Ubald was properly back in his studies Felix asked, "Why is Mr. Bookworm so dull?"

"Is he dull, my dear?"

"Yes, he went right through your fattest book, and when he came out all he could talk about was a tummy ache. Isn't that dull?"

Brother Ubald chuckled. "It's all in the mind, my dear, it's all in the mind. You can devour many books and not be a whit the wiser."

"Have I got a mind?"

"Yes, I am afraid you have," said Brother Ubald with a sigh. He had reached a very interesting part in his book.

"Then teach me how to eat books and be wiser."

"All right, dear, we'll start on the alphabet . . ."

That was how Brother Ubald acquired a pupil. Every morning Felix knocked at the library door, armed with a pencil, a sheaf of paper, and a determined frown. His tongue

was as busy as his fingers while he learned to write. The other dwarfs were delighted; it gave them some peace.

And then one day Felix's wings suddenly grew strong and bright and itched so terribly that he had to spread them.

"What are you doing?" cried Father Ubald in alarm. Felix didn't know what he was doing.

"It's my wings," he said. The next minute he was up in the air, plunging about like a top-heavy kite.

"Brother Alban, Brother Botolph—" screamed Brother Ubald. "Come and help! Felix is trying to fly!"

The other dwarfs came running.

"Take care, you'll hurt yourself!" exclaimed Brother Alban.

"You're going *straight* for the ceiling," warned Brother Botolph.

But Felix began to get the hang of it. He learned to steer himself about in the air. He found it very interesting to see everything from above. He flew through the door and up the stairs into the living room, where he surveyed the top of the table and mantelpiece. He finally got tired and took a rest on the grandfather clock.

The dwarfs had followed him. They felt uneasy.

"Don't you want to stay with us, here, safe on the ground?" they begged. "Why do you sit there? That clock hasn't been dusted for years, and you'll catch a germ, and you might fall. Besides, we get a crick in the neck looking at you."

But, like all young people, Felix disregarded those anxious cries and did exactly as nature bade him, leaning comfortably against the gold dwarf on top of the clock and swinging his legs.

Winter was over. The sun was melting the snow and coaxing back the greens. All the little streams rushed merrily downhill to spread the news that they had been let out of their prison of ice.

This was the busiest season for the forest. No one had time now to peek idly through windows and watch fairy babies grow. Mothers were airing their houses and reupholstering nests. Fathers were building and foraging. Young couples were setting up house. Courtesy was in the air. Gentlemen walked around with bouquets of primroses or forget-me-nots for the ladies. It was the time when the itch in Mr. Squirrel's legs had become unbearable, and he had suddenly vanished, leaving poor Mamma with three new babies. Luckily she had Ross, who looked after her. Scarlet and Pinkie were mad about dancing, and no use at all in the house.

Birds were arriving from the South every day; the *Forest Gazette* bristled with important names.

Miss Jenny Nightingale has arrived from Palm Beach with her nephew Lionel. She is scheduled to give her first public recital on Friday night.

Mr. and Mrs. Woodlark arrived with the evening flight. Mrs. Woodlark, née Meadowlark, wore the new French bonnet with purple strings and was much admired.

Lord and Lady Warbler will be singing their famous duet at the opera house tonight . . .

And so forth and so forth.

The best people attended the concerts and admired the new southern fashions. All day long the forest was gladdened with the sound of practicing birds.

The dwarfs opened their windows, which had been closed all winter.

At first Felix was startled at the fresh air. He drew back behind the curtains. Then he jumped on the window sill, taking deep breaths. Never had he smelled anything sweeter, more delicious, than the spring air with its scent of hyacinths and hawthorn and lilacs. The woods beckoned him; young green leaves trembled against silvery tree trunks; white dog-wood starred the mysterious depths where Felix had never been; a thrush was singing on a branch.

Felix's dark eyes glowed and shone; his cheeks reddened; and he laughed and stretched out his arms, which were already losing their chubbiness. Then he spread his gauzy wings and flew into the forest.

"Felix, Felix!" cried the dwarfs, frantic with fear. Were there not hawks and bears and wolves and eagles—all manner of dangerous creatures—abroad? And Felix, when he flew, looked a little like a dragonfly.

But Felix paid no attention. He was in ecstasy. He had discovered what he had been made for. He shot like a sun-beam through the branches, his wings shimmering and his blond curls waving about his face. Then he heard the an-guish in the voices of the dwarfs, and he returned, to be scolded and slapped and kissed and told that it wasn't safe to go into the forest.

"Safe?" asked Felix.

Brother Alban shook his head. "He doesn't understand. You tell him, Brother Ubald."

Brother Ubald tried, but danger was a thing Felix found it hard to comprehend. Quick as he had been about other things, here he was slow. Brother Ubald fingered his long beard and went to his library. From a neglected shelf he brought forth several volumes of fairy tales, and he read them to Felix.

Felix loved them, but he was not frightened of the bad wolf, nor of the bad witch, nor even of Bluebeard.

"The wolf ate the pigs, but he was nice to the little wolves, I'm sure," he said. "Perhaps the little wolves loved him very much. And the witch couldn't help being a witch when Pan made her one, could she? She had to behave like one too, poor thing. Bluebeard was bad, of course. But maybe he was going to reform, and if his wife had obeyed him they might have lived happily ever after."

As a lesson in fear, the stories were a failure.

"I don't know what we can do about it," Brother Ubald said to his brothers, "except watch him carefully."

But try to watch a young fairy lad with wings on him, when the sun is shining through the newly unfurled baby leaves of a beech tree, showing up the silver halos around the edges, and when bluebells flood the ground. The dwarfs found it impossible to keep Felix indoors. Luckily, he never flew far; mostly he sat on a branch or a flower, rocking himself and gazing into the sun.

"He is a creature of light," said Brother Ubald. "He cannot live in dark confinement, like we do. We must let him go, as long as he returns at night."

It was now Brother Botolph's turn to see the most of Felix. He made him a little spade and rake and gave him a tiny plot of land to work in.

Felix delighted in turning up the earth and encountering fellow creatures.

"Hullo," he greeted an earwig, but the earwig was deaf and went on his way without speaking.

"Don't talk to strangers," Brother Botolph warned. "It isn't nice."

Felix dug again, and a fat rainworm waddled out, grumpy at having been disturbed.

"Good morning," said Felix with his sunny smile.

"Not at all." And the rainworm wriggled off.

"Don't talk to rainworms," advised Brother Botolph. "Vulgar creatures. You'll only learn bad manners from them. Stay near me."

But Felix was too restless to do that. He flew to a low branch of the oak tree and almost landed on a green caterpillar, the exact color of the leaf. "How do you do?" he asked.

"I do as I please," mumbled the caterpillar with his mouth full.

"You see?" Brother Botolph pointed out. "It only creates unpleasantness to mix with strangers; stay here."

But that Felix could not do. The itch in his wings was even greater than the itch in Mr. Squirrel's legs. For the first time in his life he felt sad. He did not know why. He did not know that he was longing for a playmate, someone as young and eager for adventures as he was himself. No one had time for him—no one at all. The dwarfs were preoccupied. The garden had to be planted, the house had to be spring-cleaned, and the books had to be dusted (Brother Ubald had to do the last himself, or he'd never know where to find the ones he wanted).

And so Felix began to roam the forest in search of a friend. At any other time there would have been many to bid him welcome, but in spring—well, it could wait, couldn't it? Mamma Squirrel did invite him into her hole, but what with tending the babies and scolding Scarlet and Pinkie there was little chance for conversation. She was kind, however. She cracked some nuts for him and made him taste some of her acorn soup. She also let him hold the triplets and give them their bottle.

"Feeding is an important thing," she said, tenderly watching the little moving jaws. "No one would live, if he was not fed." She pondered this for a moment. "Think of all the meals, all over the world . . ." she said with awe.

Felix soon left. The hole was too narrow and dark, and he craved the sunlight. He went to look for it, flying between the smooth gray stems of beech trees flecked by the green light which filtered through the leaves. He came to an open space where the sun broke through like a golden shower. In its warmth many flowers had opened their cups and were sending forth a concert of odors. Vines curled their tendrils around them; butterflies danced over them; and in the midst sat a forlorn little creature, weeping bitterly. It had a bushy tail and white stripes on its dark back. Its large blue eyes were brimming with tears.

"What is the matter?" asked Felix. He had never seen anybody cry, and it made him feel queer.

"I have lost my mother!" wailed the creature, rubbing his paws into his long eyelashes and tangling them up.

"I have no mother either," said Felix. "Only three papas."

The little fellow gave Felix a blue stare. "I *do* have a mother," he lamented, "if I could only find her. Oh, where is she? I have had no lunch." His paws moved lower down now to indicate the empty spot.

Felix understood. Here was common ground. They both liked lunch. "What is your favorite food?" he asked.

The little creature thought, wrinkling its nose. "Honey," it said.

Felix clapped his hands and fluttered his wings. "Just what I like best!" he exclaimed. "Come home with me and my papas will give you some."

"Who are you?" asked the little creature shyly.

"I am Felix, and my papas are the dwarfs."

"Oh, the dwarfs! Oh no, I don't think I'd like to go with you. Mother says the dwarfs are mean."

Felix laughed. What an ignorant little thing it was, to be sure. "Who are you?" he asked.

"I'm Archibald," the creature answered proudly. "My father is Vincent Skunk-Phoo, not one of the common Skunks. He can trace his ancestors back to the Ark." And Archibald modestly lowered his eyelashes.

"What does he do?" asked Felix.

"He manufactures perfume," said Archibald. "He sells even to Queen Titania, and the flower fairies buy from him. It's all in the way you use a gift. I am going to be like him." And Archibald fluffed up his fur.

"It's most interesting." Felix was gazing at his new friend with admiration. "But do come and have lunch now."

"Oh no, not with the dwarfs; they're mean," said Archibald.

"Where did you get that idea?" asked Felix, astonished. "They're kind and good and all-wise. Come and see for yourself."

"Oh!" Archibald's beautiful eyes opened wide with wonder. "Really?"

"Yes, really. Come and see. There is Papa Ubald—he is very learned, you know. He does not talk much, and you must not disturb him, for that breaks his thread."

"What thread?" asked Archibald.

"He has his thoughts in his head on a thread, and if you talk to him it breaks," explained Felix. "Then he has to start a new thread all over again, and it may not be such a good one. But he is very kind, and he almost never gets angry."

"And who else is there?" asked Archibald.

"Papa Alban. He is very often angry, but he does not mean it; it's just his nerves. He likes me to stroke his head, because he has headaches. He makes lovely food and he is always busy looking after us. Then there is Papa Botolph. He is fun. He collects the most beautiful eggshells, and he makes flowers and salads and smells of onions and parsley. He plays games sometimes. But when you are hurt it is best to go to Papa Alban—he can take it away."

Curiosity was overcoming Archibald's fears. Besides, he was hungry. "All right, I'll go with you," he consented graciously.

Overjoyed, Felix took his paw. "Come, then," he said tenderly. "I will show you the way. Don't be afraid of the dark forest; the sun is right behind the trees all the time."

"I know *that*," protested Archibald, piqued. "I *live* in this forest."

"How did you get lost, then?" asked Felix.

Archibald seemed embarrassed by this question. The fact

was that he had been disobedient. He preferred not to think of it, and changed the subject. "What shall we have for lunch?" he asked.

The dwarfs had eaten their lunch and had left Felix's plate on the table. Brother Alban was annoyed that he hadn't come in time for the meal and muttered to himself that life was becoming impossible and that there seemed no end to what he had to put up with. His brothers had missed Felix's gay chatter and were out of humor too.

Brother Botolph was the first to catch sight of the culprit, hand in hand with a skunk.

"Great Pan have mercy on us," he muttered. "Look at that."

He went to warn his brothers. "Here's that child, bringing home a skunk!"

"Don't let him in!" screeched Brother Alban, waving a saucepan.

"Don't stop him, you mean," came Brother Ubald's quiet voice. "He'll do no harm as long as we don't frighten or anger him. Keep calm, everybody, keep calm."

The dwarfs trembled with anticipation.

"Hullo!" cried Felix, jumping into the kitchen and bestowing radiant smiles on the dwarfs. "Here's Archibald, who has lost his mother. Can he have some lunch?"

Brother Alban bit his lips.

"Certainly," said Brother Ubald.

Felix hadn't waited for permission. "Here," he told Archibald, who was staring at the dwarfs. "Here, you may sit in my chair and have my plate and spoon." He ran off to the pantry and came staggering back with a huge jar of honey. "It's our best crocus honey," he announced. "Papa Botolph made it. Or would you rather have hyacinth honey? It's a bit peppery. But try it." He darted off to get some.

Brother Alban and Brother Botolph exchanged agonized glances. Not only did Felix reappear with the hyacinth honey, but he brought in the dessert Brother Alban had prepared for dinner, and some of the best maple candy.

The three brothers looked on helplessly while Archibald dug into his feast. Felix watched him from the other end of the table, his chin resting on his folded arms and his face one bright beam of hospitality.

"Isn't it nice?" he asked. "Isn't Papa Alban good at cooking? Do you see now that the dwarfs aren't mean? Do you see how kind they are?" He was much too excited to eat himself. "And, you know, Papa Ubald is very clever. He knows *everything*. Ask him a question now, do! He knows the answer to them all."

Archibald mumbled something with his mouth full.

"He wants to know why he can't eat the moon," Felix interpreted.

The dwarfs cast up their eyes at such an insatiable appetite. Brother Ubald obediently launched into a lengthy scientific description of the size and composition of the moon,

but Archibald wasn't listening. He had finished the two jars of honey, the cranberry pie, and the plate full of candy.

"Can I have some more?" he asked.

Brother Alban was going to shriek *"No-o-o!"* when Brother Botolph stamped hard on his foot, making him yelp, *"Ouch!"* instead.

Frowning, the dwarfs watched Archibald dig into a beautiful bit of dandelion cheese, made out of the milk that oozes from dandelion stalks. (It's rather bitter, and you have to get used to it, but the dwarfs like nothing better.)

"Papa Alban made that," Felix announced proudly.

Archibald took another slice.

Brother Alban vented his anger by punching Brother Ubald in the ribs. Brother Ubald had his nose in a thick book called *The Psychical Disturbances and Neurotic Symptoms of the Skunk Family*. He gave a howl of pain.

"What's the matter?" asked Archibald, between chews.

"Nothing, nothing," Brother Ubald answered hastily.

As Archibald's appetite diminished, his curiosity rose. "Can you wiggle your ears?" he asked.

Brother Ubald disclaimed any such powers.

"I can wiggle my teeth," Archibald told him, moving a loose baby tooth from side to side.

"Brother Alban can roll his eyes," Felix boasted.

"Oh, lemme see!" begged Archibald.

Brother Alban blushed uncomfortably. He did not want to perform before the unwelcome visitor, but Brother Botolph gave him a push from behind.

"Lemme see, lemme see," whined Archibald. Felix looked up expectantly. Brother Botolph gave Brother Alban another push.

Brother Alban rolled his eyes.

Archibald clapped his paws in rapture. "Do it again!"

Brother Alban did it again.

"And Brother Botolph can whistle," said Felix, proud of Brother Alban's success and fearful lest Brother Botolph feel left out. This time it was Brother Alban's turn to push Brother Botolph. He did this with such vigor that Brother Botolph had difficulty in remaining upright.

"Lemme hear," whined Archibald, still chewing. The dwarfs thought that the food must soon be coming out of his ears. "Lemme hear!"

So Brother Botolph whistled.

"Do it again!"

Brother Botolph did it again. Then, looking at the greatly diminished supply of cheese, he asked, "Are you sure you have had enough?"

Archibald reluctantly admitted that he could not eat any more. "Perhaps if I ran around a bit . . ." he suggested, but the dwarfs assured him that it was very bad to go on eating after you've had enough.

"Then I'll be going home," announced Archibald, who had not yet come to the age when one feels it is impolite to leave right after a meal.

"Indeed, we quite understand," the dwarfs assured him. "Don't let us keep you."

"Come on, Felix," said Archibald.

"Felix stays here," Brother Alban began.

Archibald's face puckered. His blue eyes filled with tears. "I must have Felix!" he wailed.

"Oh, all right, all right." The dwarfs hastily consented.

Felix and Archibald danced out into the sunlight to look for Archibald's mother.

They found the mother busily looking for Archibald.

"Oh, Mother, I've made such a lovely friend!" cried Archibald, rushing into her outstretched paws with flying tail. "Here he is; his name is Felix; and he lives with the dwarfs. They are not a bit mean, Mother—they have a beautiful house with a staircase in it, and they have lots of food. You should have *seen* it, Mother!"

Archibald's mother was agreeably surprised. She was gracious to Felix and thanked him for helping her little son. Later she told the neighbors, "It just shows you that you must never judge people. I always thought those dwarfs the most ill-mannered and selfish folk I'd ever met, and here they were so kind to Archibald. It makes me feel ashamed of myself. Vincent and I are going to pay them a call."

So they did, decked in their best clothes and carrying printed cards, in case the dwarfs weren't home. Of course the dwarfs *were* home, and not at all pleased to see them, but there was nothing for it except to be agreeable again. Mr. Skunk-Phoo was all Archibald had boasted that he was. He wore a top hat and a monocle and he used very long words. His wife was most elegantly attired—she wore white gloves and carried a handkerchief drenched in her husband's most expensive perfume.

Brother Alban served camomile tea and caraway cookies. He did not know what to say, and conversation would have flagged if it had not been for Felix, who chattered away about the dwarfs' perfections and the amiable characteristics of Archibald till everyone was pleased and even the dwarfs began to believe in their own hospitality.

This, of course, was a social event. The Skunk-Phoos

didn't visit just anybody. It was mentioned in the *Forest Gazette,* and the dwarfs were absurdly pleased.

It has come to our ears that Mr. and Mrs. Vincent Skunk-Phoo have been entertained by the Brothers McOakum, our estimable dwarfs. We have it on good authority that Mrs. Skunk-Phoo wore a lilac gown trimmed with gray fur and had one of the newest hats perched lightly over the left ear. We congratulate the brothers on a very successful tea party.

Brother Alban and Brother Botolph hung over Brother

Ubald's shoulder while he read it out again and again.

The trouble about a reputation is that it is hard to live down. The dwarfs had now been publicly commended for their hospitality. They could no longer slam the door in the faces of casual visitors. They realized this themselves. Nor would they have cared to disillusion Felix, who went around telling everybody what good fellows they were. Now the dwarfs had never suffered much from their bad reputation, but they found that a good reputation can become a very expensive and troublesome luxury. If it hadn't been for Felix, of course, the situation might not have been so bad. But Felix made altogether too many friends. The dwarfs began to feel they had no home any longer. Whenever Brother Ubald wanted to sit down and read he was sure to find some animal curled up in his chair. Brother Alban never knew how many would come for the meals, and was constantly wiping up dirty footmarks. As for Brother Botolph, Felix's friendly relations with rabbits, chipmunks, woodchucks, and squirrels were so inconvenient that he began to long for the good old days of the alarm clock.

Of course the dwarfs protested. They told Felix what they felt about his friends. They told him how much they liked privacy and peace. They told him that they liked to eat their own food once in a while. But Felix smiled as if to say, "You may grumble, but I know you love all these creatures just as much as I do." And what can one do against a belief like that?

4. The King's Message

Felix felt very sorry for Mamma Squirrel. She had been kind
to him all summer, and the triplets had been fun to play
with, but obviously Mr. Squirrel's absence was beginning to
prey on her. She was losing her healthy red color and becoming pale. Her eyes were swollen from weeping.

"I can't imagine what has happened to him," she moaned,
rocking one of the triplets on her lap. "You'd think he would
at least have sent me word. It's almost eight weeks now since
he went. He might be dead, and I none the wiser. It's the
worry and the uncertainty I mind most. If I knew he was
happy, I would not fret. But how can he be happy? Who

67

else knows the way he likes his coffee and his nuts prepared? Who else will make his bed the way he wants it, without a wrinkle and with a balsam pillow? I fear very much that he is miserable—but ashamed to come back because he thinks I am angry." (Here Mrs. Squirrel wiped her eyes with the tail of the triplet she was holding on her lap.)

She continued in the tenderest of tones. "Angry—how can I be angry when I love him? Poor Red, alone and desolate, while we are longing for him. But how can I let him know? It is very sad." And she sobbed quietly.

Felix wished he could help her. He had grown a lot during the summer, and tears were no longer a novelty to him. He had shared the grief of Mrs. Hare when her eldest son had blundered into a trap and had suffered a cruel death. He had helped when a storm blew down one of the oldest trees in the forest, causing untold havoc and misery and filling the *Forest Gazette* with the names of its wounded inhabitants. He also regularly visited the poor old witch in the forest hospital who had been knocked silly by lightning and had forgotten all her spells. He talked to her about cats and broomsticks, and that made her feel at home.

He was less and less with the dwarfs now, and they were complaining.

"Wouldn't you rather be here," they asked, "with your papas, instead of gallivanting all over the forest?"

They did not understand about the itch in his wings. He tried to explain it. "I like it here very much," he would tell

them. "But the sky is so blue, and there are delightful little clouds up there, softer than a bed. It's fun, too, to sit on the treetops. You meet interesting people. Do you know what Jack Crow told me?"

And he would launch into the latest forest gossip.

"Poor Mrs. Powderpuff's son is ill. He ate a poisonous mushroom, and they are very worried. She has too many children to mind, she says, but Jack Crow says it's because she reads comic books instead of doing her duty. Mr. Hoot has been made an honorary doctor by King Oberon. The king's messenger came himself, in a gold uniform, and the diploma was tied with scarlet ribbons and had a gold seal. I wish I had seen him. The mice say it's quite undeserved, but I don't think so, for he looks like a wise old owl. And the king should know, shouldn't he?"

Willy-nilly, the dwarfs grew interested and would sometimes ask of their own accord, "Did Mrs. Powderpuff's son recover? How is Dr. Hoot today?"

But not even the flying about and making friends quite succeeded in curing the itch in Felix's wings. No one who has not experienced it can understand what it feels like. It is a thirst, an appetite, a longing, and yet none of these things. For there is no food, nor drink, nor possession that can fill it. It seems to push at you, and pull at you, but you don't know where it wants you to go. And the strangest thing is that you know that what you want is not something new, but something very, very old; not something foreign, but very, very familiar—only you've forgotten what it is.

Poor Felix suffered with it. He no longer sought friends; he avoided them. He went for long walks in the wood, hoping that perhaps if he smelled the right smell, he'd remember—for our noses have the best memory of all.

There are woods and woods. Some are like halls, or churches with russet carpets of dead leaves—smooth columns of trees holding up a stately vaulted roof. Then there are scrappy brushwoods, young and green and sappy, harboring little snakes and many nests, like new, suburban villas. Or there are the dense pine jungles, protected by the spikes of dead branches, with never a bit of green to relieve the gray—the favorite haunts of spiders, who stretch out their webs and sit there, waiting for foolish little flies. Those woods are like the financial section of a big metropolis.

Felix knew all the different parts of the forest, yet one day, mysteriously, he got lost.

He was following a scent—he was smelling something that reminded him of what he was looking for. He wandered on and on. It seemed to him that the scent was getting stronger. He came to where he had never been before—a deep cavern of foliage growing darker and darker and more silent as the moss grew thicker and vines slung themselves more luxuriantly from tree to tree, hindering the sun. No matter where Felix turned, he met strangeness, mystery. It seemed as if the air grew colder, thinner, stiller. There were no more throbbing insects. Even the twigs refused to crackle. Felix had never been frightened before. He forgot the scent in his panic to get back to familiar surroundings. But the more he tried to break away, the deeper he seemed to penetrate into the eerie darkness.

Felix began to feel less and less real. He wondered whether he were dreaming. He was shivering.

There was a rustling as of an enormous snake, and Felix almost screamed as he saw two red fiery eyes gleam from the darkness and heard a sudden hiss as steaming breath left a wide nostril surrounded by green scales.

Felix closed his eyes for a moment and gave himself up for lost. It was the dragon that sometimes invaded the forest, its most dangerous enemy. Felix had heard of him but never met him. What could he do alone, unarmed, against this monster? He thought of the dwarfs, of King Oberon. The dragon opened his enormous mouth, and a red glare lit up the trees.

"Pan, help me," whimpered Felix.

And then the most beautiful sound Felix had ever heard thrilled through the forest—the clarion call of a horn, the horn of King Oberon's knights. There was a thundering sound of many hoofs, the clash of steel. The dragon closed his mouth. His fiery eye disappeared as with a slithering sound he gently retreated. And as he went, the light came back into the forest—a beautiful, silvery light, a magic light. Felix stood leaning forward, his arm around a small birch tree. His heart beat joyfully. All around him insects began to hum, birds began to sing, and animals came pattering on hurried feet.

There was a cry of, "King Oberon! King Oberon!"

Felix had forgotten the dragon. He pulled himself into the birch tree to see better. More and more animals appeared, forming a line. There was another trumpet call, and then, to the music of cymbals and bells, the flower fairies came into view, dressed in the tenderest of pastel-colored gowns, with wreaths in their long silky hair, as they danced along, scattering flower petals.

Next came the king's pages, fairies no older than Felix in little white suits with gold capes. They played on small reed flutes. And then came the knights on prancing white-winged

horses, with silver armor that seemed to cast a glow around it. They carried swords and spears and banners; their shields carried King Oberon's crest; the plumes on their helmets were white and gold. Then came the heralds in crimson velvet on black horses, and finally, drawn by four white ponies in a crystal coach, the king and the queen.

The forest echoed and re-echoed with the cheers of the spectators. The king was noble and handsome. Long brown curls flowed from under his crown; his eyes were clear and blue; his brown beard partly hid a warm smile. The queen sat beside him, her small head held high on a long neck, which was adorned with glittering jewels. A small diadem perched on her dark hair. The scarlet of the king's robes against the gold and white of the queen's gown made a gay splash, and all the colors glittered and shone in the rainbow reflections from the crystal carriage.

The itch in Felix's wings had grown very bad.

The king held up his hand, and suddenly the procession stopped. "Felix," said the king. "Come here."

Wondering mightily, Felix slid out of the tree and came forward. All the animals looked at him. The horses tossed their heads and champed on their bits.

"Do not be afraid," said King Oberon. "Come here." Felix came as close to the coach as he dared. He suddenly realized that his hands and knees were dirty, that there were twigs in his uncombed hair, and that his tunic was torn.

"Tell me," asked the king, "are you happy?"

"Yes, oh yes, Your Majesty," stammered Felix. "My papas are good to me and I have many friends. I am very happy—but just now I was afraid. I saw a dragon—"

The king's face grew grim. "I know," he said. "My knights will deal with him presently. Now we are concerned about you. You are sure you are happy?"

"Yes, when my wings don't itch."

The king looked at him tenderly. "Do they itch sometimes?"

"A little," confessed Felix. "Flying helps."

King Oberon put his hand on Felix's shoulders where the wings were fastened, and a gentle, glowing warmth stole through Felix's body. The itching stopped. "If it should get unbearable, and flying does not help any more, you may use this," the king told him, handing him a little gold key. "It will open the palace door. You will be welcome."

Felix now dared to look up at the smiling face of King Oberon. Behind him the queen nodded graciously. He could smell the soft perfume from her hair. Felix wanted to be there forever and ever, with the two of them, but already the king had made the signal for his procession to continue.

"Where is the palace?" asked Felix hurriedly. "How can I find it—and when?"

"That will be shown to you later," the king promised. "As soon as you need it." The coachman cracked his whip, the heralds blew their horns, the forest folk cheered, and the procession was on its way again, soon vanishing among the trees. The last they heard was the sound of hoofs and the tinkle of bells, slowly fading.

Felix had to answer some questions from bystanders who were curious as to what the king had said. He did not tell them much, because he wanted to think over quietly what had happened. Most of the animals were hurrying to another point of vantage where they might see the procession again, and Felix soon stood alone.

He was overwhelmed with the honor done to him. He stared at the little key in his hands. It was made of exquisite filigree, a truly royal key. Looking up, he saw that the fairy light was fading. Every moment the forest was looking more normal. Fingering his key, he walked confidently and soon recognized his surroundings. How could he have got lost like that? Thoughtfully he walked on. It had seemed to him that he had been gone for a long time, yet the sun slanted at almost the same degree through the trees. Could it be that hardly any time had elapsed?

Or had he fallen asleep and dreamed it all?

He had come to a rather wild and uncivilized part of the forest, which he had not visited often, as the dwarfs had told him he might meet unpleasant creatures there. It was the favorite spot of the more mischievous fairies, and it was rumored that witches held a sort of fair there, frequented by the lower kind of animals. Others said that this was not true at all—that, on the contrary, it was a dull place.

Felix now came upon it accidentally, as he was finding

his way home. He looked about curiously but saw nothing unusual. A field mouse was industriously cleaning the front of her house, two moles were gossiping over their market baskets, and an old witch was gathering herbs. Felix felt slightly disappointed. Then a sound aroused his curiosity. Someone was singing. This is what he heard.

> "Rumty-um, I am a bad man,
> A bad, wicked man am I.
> I left my wee wife and my babies three
> To go rioting on the sly—
>   Oh why?
> To go rioting on the sly."

Felix could not see the singer until he had rounded a clump of holly. Then he halted in surprise. He saw Mr. Red

Squirrel lying on his back under a beech tree, his legs crossed and one foot kicking up and down as he sang.

Felix felt shocked. He remembered Mamma Squirrel's grief, and here was her wretch of a husband singing. Would it be better to pretend not to see him? Or was it his duty to deliver Mamma's message—though Mr. Squirrel seemed scarcely in the humor to appreciate it?

"Hullo," he said.

"Oh, hullo, hullo, hullo." Mr. Squirrel scrambled into a sitting position. "Oh, it's the little orphan! Humph. Please excuse me—I—er—didn't comb my fur this morning. Do sit down. The moss here is soft."

Felix, however, remained standing. "Ross is very anxious about you," was all he said.

"Ah, er—yes—Ross—." Mr. Squirrel toyed with his tail.

"So are Scarlet and Pinkie," Felix continued. "And Mamma and the triplets."

"Yes, yes, no doubt." Mr. Squirrel cleared his throat. "I—er—played hooky—Got fed up. Happens sometimes. You're too young to know." He shifted his position.

"Don't you think you ought to come home?"

"Perhaps I should . . . perhaps I should . . . ," Mr. Squirrel agreed. "There are times when the forest palls too. I may as well confess to you that I am a failure," he added in a burst of confidence.

Felix sat down with his arms around humped knees. "What is that—a failure?"

"A failure is a person who does not live up to his own expectations," said Mr. Squirrel.

"And what were your expectations?" asked Felix.

"Aaaaaah!" Mr. Squirrel stretched himself on his back again and shut his eyes. "I had wonderful expectations," he admitted. "I wanted to be a knight in armor and kill a dragon. I wanted to marry a princess. None of these things did I do. So, you see, I am a failure."

Felix's eyes glittered. "Have you ever seen a dragon?" he asked in a low voice, glancing behind him for a moment.

"Not exactly," said Mr. Squirrel, "but I know what they're like. The thing to do is to hit them in the eye—that's their vulnerable spot—and then—ker-bing!" And he lunged with a stick.

Felix remembered a terrible red eye and shuddered. "Dragons are dangerous," he said with awe in his voice. "And knights have to be very brave and splendid."

"Naturally, naturally," agreed Mr. Squirrel, chewing on a blade of grass. "Why else do you think I want to be one?" And he flicked a bit of moss from his coat.

"But you're a squirrel," protested Felix. "Squirrels don't become knights, and they couldn't slay dragons and marry princesses."

"Couldn't they?" asked Mr. Squirrel. "If they wanted to very badly, couldn't they?"

"Well, I don't believe so," said Felix.

"Then why do I want to do it; why do I keep thinking

about it and thinking about it—seeing myself in armor, charging on a horse, gallumpity, gallumpity, till I meet a monster, a big scaly monster, and out comes my sword. . . . The monster is clasping a beautiful little squirrel . . . her eyes are wet with tears. . . . Then she sees me . . . her eyes light up . . . I come . . . the monster opens his mouth, but I pierce his tongue with my sword. He collapses in a pool of blood. I look around for the lady squirrel . . . she has fainted. . . . Aaaah." Mr. Squirrel sank back onto the moss after excited gesticulations. "Why does it never happen?"

"Do you really want it to happen?" asked Felix, who had listened, enthralled. "Or do you just want to *think* about it? For if you only want to think about it you must be a poet— that's what poets do. Why don't you write a book?"

Mr. Squirrel sat up. His hair bristled. He breathed fast. His eyes twinkled like anthracite. "That's it; you've got it!" he said. "I always knew I was not like the others! Now I do not have to be a failure. I shall rescue my lady and fight my battles in books. It's more convenient too—it takes less *out* of one, in a manner of speaking. All I need now is paper."

"You can get that off the birch trees," said Felix.

Mr. Squirrel rubbed his paws together with satisfaction. "Yes, my boy, we'll write, we'll write," he muttered, delighted with himself. "That's it, of course—a poet. I am a poet. Why did I not think of it before? If Mamma says, 'Why did you go away, Red?' I shall answer, 'To compose poetry.' Beautiful."

"That would not be quite true, would it?" asked Felix.

"It would, and it wouldn't. I went away to slay a dragon, and you have just told me yourself that that is poetry. Very well, poetry it is."

Mr. Squirrel was in high good humor. There wasn't a trace of the penitent about him. He accompanied Felix home, and whenever they were not chattering Mr. Squirrel hummed and twirled his stick.

Mamma Squirrel saw her husband from afar and ran to meet him. She fell on his neck and kissed him. Not one word of reproach did she utter. Mr. Squirrel was touched. He had tears in his eyes. The triplets had run after their mother and stood staring at him, their tails in their mouths. Ross, Scarlet, and Pinkie came shyly behind.

Mr. Squirrel patted his wife, and then he patted his children. "So, rumpty-um," he said. "So—so. Glad to be home and all that. Humph. Very glad indeed." And he put his arm around Mamma Squirrel's shoulders. Then the happy, reunited family filed into their hole to celebrate.

Felix spread his wings and flew home, smiling.

The summer slowly faded, and autumn came again, stripping the trees. It was a colder, sadder autumn this year. There was more of brown and gray in it and less of scarlet. Many of the nutshells were empty, the toadstools had queer shapes, and spiders abounded.

But Mamma Squirrel felt happy.

Mr. Squirrel did not go roving any more. He had built himself a study and sat writing there all day. It was true that when she came to bring him his coffee he barely noticed her and she had to watch that he did not dip his pen in the coffee and drink the ink; it was also true that she had to keep the children quiet and away from their father. But at least she knew where he was and that he was happy, and there was always Ross—dear Ross—to do the chores for her. Also, there were the wonderful moments when Mr. Squirrel would come into her living room, fling himself on the sofa, and groan, "I'm a failure, I'm a failure," and allow her to pet him.

So she was very, very grateful to Felix for having suggested that Mr. Squirrel write a book. His writing must be good, for he'd had two poems accepted by the *Gazette*. He was now writing the memoirs of his travels. Mamma Squirrel was very curious as to what there could be to write about. She would have liked very much to read them, but he would not allow it. The only bits she could find were the crumpled sheets in the wastepaper basket, which she smoothed out and read. These astonished her exceedingly and made her wish she could read the in-between bits. This was the sort of thing she found:

"Knave," I hissed between my teeth, "put down that dagger, or I'd fain pierce thee." The villain glared at me between lowered brows. Well did I know his breed, and I drew the sword from my scabbard. The villain lunged at me with his dagger, but my

sword was longer. When I had disposed of him I wiped my
sword and went on.

Or:

"Prithee, have mercy, sire," the damsel said. She was passing
fair to look upon, and my heart was moved.

"Nay, grieve not," I told her. "I am a knight, not a monster.
Come and sup with me." But she blushed modestly and whispered, "Sire—my mother is ill."

"Well, then, go in peace," I told her with a sigh.

Mamma Squirrel marveled at it all. "No wonder he did
not want to stay home," she whispered. "And how nice that
that lady loved her mother." She told the children not to
make any noise.

"Your father is a hero," she warned, "though you might not have guessed it. He is writing it all down, and I won't have him disturbed. You shall hear his adventures when they are published."

She considered herself the most fortunate of women. Of course, Felix was her favorite visitor. Nothing was ever too good for him. She declared that his bright face was enough to bring anyone luck.

There were others who shared that opinion—there wasn't a creature in the forest who disliked Felix. He was welcome everywhere.

One evening when the dwarfs were enjoying a quiet supper of corn mush, stewed mushrooms, and elderberry wine, Felix came flying into the house, blazing with excitement. "Do you know what Mamma Squirrel told me?" he cried, clapping his hands. "There's going to be a party here in the forest, a wonderful party, and it's called Halloween! Everybody is going, and I want to go too! I've thought of a costume already; I want to dress up as a firefly!"

The dwarfs sat stiff and still. Their eyes were cast down.

"What's the matter?" asked Felix. "It will be quite safe, you know. Mr. Squirrel has promised I may join his group, and the Skunk-Phoos have invited me too. They are all going—even Professor Hoot. It is *everyone's* party—you can come too. We are going to dress up and knock at people's doors and cry 'tricks or treats.' And then—do you know what will happen then? We'll get apples and nuts and all sorts of other nice foods. Mamma Squirrel says Ross fetched her a month's supply last year." Felix looked around, expecting to see glad, or at least tolerant, smiles. But instead he saw the same wooden faces.

"Don't you *like* Halloween?" he asked, astonished.

Brother Alban cleared his throat. "Do you see now," he said in a voice vibrant with emotion, while he banged his fist on the table. "Do you see now the trick they played on us? They counted on that innocent child, they counted on our affection for him, to get the better of us. If you want to be fools, go ahead. But count me out." And he left the table.

"Yes," said Brother Botolph, "I agree. Count me out too."

Only Brother Ubald remained sitting at the table. He looked very sad.

"What's the matter?" asked Felix. "Can't I go?"

"Son," said Brother Ubald tenderly, "sit on my knee and I shall try to explain it to you. You see, long, long ago, before you were born, your papas had trouble with the other forest people. Your papas believed that they should be free to live their own lives, unmolested by the demands and pleasures of others." Here Brother Ubald stopped to blow his nose. "The forest people don't agree with us. They say we belong to them. They want us to pay taxes in the form of nuts and apples, and partake of their vulgar gaiety. Therefore a feud has developed. We cannot possibly let you join the forest people at Halloween. It would be like joining the enemy."

"But they're not enemies!" cried Felix, bewildered.

He remembered the cozy stove in Mamma Squirrel's hole, and she herself sitting beside it, knitting socks for the triplets, who were asleep in their beds. He remembered Mr. Squirrel with his slippers on and his feet on the mantelpiece, reading the *Forest Gazette*. He also remembered Mrs. Skunk-Phoo's boudoir, with Mrs. Skunk-Phoo sitting in front of her mirror while Miss Rosie Chipmunk, her maid, brushed her hair and Archibald hunted in her drawers and boxes for bonbons—and poor Mrs. Powderpuff's home, with all the children fighting and quarreling on the dirty floor while she, in a tattered pink kimono, sat curled up on the sofa, reading comics.

"They are not enemies," he said.

"You don't understand," Brother Ubald explained sadly. "There are things little children have to accept from their elders. I'm afraid we'll have to forbid you to go to this party. You'll have to stay with us. Brother Alban always closes up the house so we can't hear or see anything. It is, I'm afraid, a dull and tiresome evening."

"Oh, Papa Ubald," said Felix, tears springing into his eyes, "they will all be so disappointed! I promised to help the chipmunks with their costumes; Mamma Squirrel wants me to keep an eye on the triplets for her; Professor Hoot said he'd lend me a lantern if I'd curl his wig for him. And I promised everyone that you'd give plenty of apples and nuts, because Papa Botolph has had such a good harvest. What shall I say to them? They're my *friends*."

Brother Ubald stroked his beard and looked at Felix pensively. "It's hard luck," he admitted. "But I'm afraid you can't go."

Felix could not understand it. He naturally believed that the dwarfs knew best; he did not question their judgment; but it puzzled and saddened him.

All over the forest his friends were preparing for the party. They asked Felix to admire their costumes, they begged for his help, they shared their plans with him—in fact, they chattered of nothing else. Felix tried to echo their gaiety, but tears kept pricking in his eyes. He no longer re-counted his forest adventures at home—what was there to tell that would please the dwarfs? And he no longer mentioned the dwarfs to his friends—why hurt their feelings? He thought more and more about his meeting with the king.

He became quiet and pensive and suddenly grew taller. His cheeks lost their roundness and pink color. The dwarfs noticed it, but it did not alter their resolution.

"It's only a child's whim," they said. "He'll get over it."

On Halloween night they would not let Felix out of their sight, though he had shown no spirit of rebellion. The temptation to sneak out might prove too much for him. They locked the door as usual and closed the shutters. Felix complained of a headache—a very unusual malady for a fairy—so they sent him to bed. Brother Ubald felt anxious about him and put an extra blanket over him. Several times that evening one of the dwarfs went to look at him. He was lying very still and pale, with his eyes shut.

Presently there was the usual knocking on the door, and the dwarfs remembered their former quarrel with the forest, but it was a tame night. Nothing exciting happened—no shaking of the tree, no eerie noises, no laughter.

"I think we have beaten them!" Brother Alban cried triumphantly. "They see their tricks didn't work. Now we can go to bed."

"First let's look once more at Felix, poor boy," said Brother Ubald, taking the candle and mounting the winding stairs to Felix's bedroom. But when he opened the door he gasped, and the candle almost dropped out of his hand. "Felix is gone!" he exclaimed.

"Gone? But the door was locked. That can't have happened!" the others protested.

They rushed into the room. It *had* happened. Felix's bed was empty, and no matter how the dwarfs searched and called, they could not find him. Felix had vanished as mysteriously as he had come.

5. Sickness and Sorrow

Mr. Squirrel didn't enjoy this Halloween as much as he had the last one. Pretty Miss Rosie Chipmunk had got herself engaged to a rather dull fellow, a cousin, and would dance with no one else. The weather was damp and chilly. There were too many spiders and not enough glowworms. (It is impossible to realize what this means unless you know both intimately. Without wanting to detract from spiders, who are excellent and virtuous creatures in their own way, one must admit that they have sour dispositions and are not given to affectionate gaiety. Glowworms, on the other hand, are cordial fellows who can make a feast out of a funeral.)

The fairies didn't dance, and left before midnight; the only witch who arrived had a cold, kept sneezing, and refused to fly on her broomstick because she said it was hard on the lungs. The food was poor and there wasn't enough elderberry wine to make a mouse merry. Something had gone wrong with the forest, whatever it was.

Everyone felt it.

No one was gay.

Oh yes, there were the usual handouts, but presents aren't enough to make a party; there must be a spirit of friendship, the wish to be together and to celebrate. This year the most intimate friends seemed strangers.

"Come on, Ross," Mr. Squirrel said finally, after having waited in vain for the evening to warm up, "let's go home to Mamma."

A slight drizzle wetted their coats. Other people were going home too.

"Why wasn't Felix there?" asked Ross.

Mr. Squirrel stood still. Of course, that was it—why hadn't he thought of it before?—he'd missed Felix. Yet last year Felix had not been there either, so to speak! That's why he hadn't realized it.

"Why wasn't he?" Ross repeated.

Mr. Squirrel didn't know. "Perhaps he is ill . . . or something happened to the dwarfs . . ."

"Listen," said Ross. They heard a faint call echoing through the wood, and saw three threads of light, wavering threads, that terminated in luminous points. These points bobbed up and down, and the threads of light wandered about drunkenly, now parallel, now crisscrossing.

"Lanterns," said Ross.

"Whose lanterns?" asked Mr. Squirrel.

"Listen," said Ross.

They could faintly hear a call of "Felix—Felix—"

"It's the dwarfs. That means Felix is not home. Let's find out what's the matter," proposed Ross. The two squirrels ran to meet the lanterns.

And that's how the forest folk found out what had happened. For this was not another trick of the animals. Whatever had caused Felix's disappearance, the forest had had nothing to do with it. Felix was a universal favorite, and the dwarfs were not alone in their grief. Nor were they alone in their search for Felix. The *Gazette* came out with black borders the next day, and an editorial about the lost fairy. A reward was promised to whoever brought him back. It was rumored that this reward would be paid by Mr. Skunk-Phoo, president of the Prudential Perfume Company (though this was to be kept a secret). However, no efforts succeeded in retrieving Felix, though there were plenty of false alarms. Obscure little animals such as groundhogs and field mice would come hopefully with worthless "clues," their tiny eyes glistening with greed for the reward. There were constant whispers about someone who had spoken to somebody who had seen Felix somewhere! But it never led

to anything. It only unsettled the dwarfs and kept them in a state of constant expectation and disappointment.

Gradually hopes faded. The forest began to mourn its loss. The few leaves left on the trees turned black at the edges. Chokecherries and other berries turned black too, and Mrs. Powderpuff called her new baby Sympathy.

And so the dwarfs were left alone again—free to read, free to be tidy, free to be quiet and alone. But, like the contrary creatures they were, they now wept for the happy days when little footsteps sounded in or around the house; when a little fairy voice hummed tunes; when the rustle of wings filled the passage and two slender arms would go around their necks in the warmest of fairy hugs.

"I never knew I'd miss him so," sobbed Brother Alban, letting big tears fall into the soup.

"What's the use of reading when there's no one to ask me questions?" Brother Ubald sighed, wiping his glasses for the hundredth time.

"Why should I plant bulbs when he isn't there to pick the flowers?" wailed Brother Botolph, blowing his nose.

Somehow all the zest had gone out of the dwarfs' lives. They had got accustomed to someone who ran in and out of their house and brought them news of the forest. They felt lonely. They wondered how they had ever been content without Felix.

When Brother Alban found a pair of Felix's shoes behind the stove he gilded them and put them on the mantelpiece

under a glass cover with a sprig of dried forget-me-nots pasted on it.

When Brother Botolph found a lock of Felix's hair hanging from a thorn bush he made a ring out of it which he wore on his little finger.

When Brother Ubald found a dirty footprint of Felix's on the library carpet he would not let Brother Alban clean it up. He put a little fence around it instead, to protect it. And often he would sit in his chair and gaze at it tearfully.

Of course the three brothers talked it all over endlessly. Why had Felix left? Had he gone by himself or had he been taken?

"If only he is well and looked after!" Brother Botolph sighed.

"I hope someone washes his clothes and feeds him," moaned Brother Alban.

"Perhaps he didn't believe we loved him," murmured Brother Ubald. As he had read the most, he could think the best. "Do you know," he said, "I believe it is our own fault. We never were grateful for Felix. We kept complaining. We never appreciated him—his cheerfulness, his affection."

"That is true." The brothers nodded sadly.

"Besides," said Brother Ubald, putting his finger to his nose and looking very wise, "I believe Felix was the sort of fairy who *has* to be friends with everyone. When we forced him to share our quarrel, he could not live."

"It is possible," sobbed the brothers.

"Perhaps, come to think of it, we've been rather selfish," Brother Ubald continued relentlessly. "Selfish and obstinate." There was a silence. Brother Botolph and Brother Alban were blushing.

But all this remorse did not bring Felix back. And the days were dreary without him. The dwarfs lost their appetites and became pale and wan.

Brother Alban suffered the most. "I don't know what it is," he said. "I seem to have no energy any more. I can hardly get through the day's work, and my head aches dreadfully."

The others thought it was just Brother Alban's usual play for sympathy; they realized that something was seriously wrong only when Brother Alban fainted dead away in the middle of frying a delicious mushroom omelette. Brother Botolph rescued the omelette, which was burning, while Brother Ubald poured water on Brother Alban. It took quite a lot of water and rubbing and shaking to bring Brother Alban to, and even then he wasn't fit for anything but to be put to bed.

The other dwarfs were in a state about it. Brother Alban had never been ill before. They were lost without him. They decided to call in Dr. Gray Owl, a cousin of Professor Hoot. Dr. Gray Owl made a careful examination of Brother Alban and prescribed complete rest for at least a month.

"It's overwork, and worry," he said. "The heart isn't what it should be. Take care of him."

Brother Ubald and Brother Botolph looked at each other in consternation. They could not take care of themselves, let alone of Brother Alban. For the first time they realized how much work that little dwarf had accomplished.

"We should have helped him more," Brother Ubald muttered remorsefully. "Then he would not have got ill. We've been selfish."

"Well, let's make it up to him now," proposed Brother Botolph. "If I only knew *how*." He sneaked up to Brother Alban's bedside, fluffed his pillows, and gazed at him affectionately, but Brother Alban was too far gone to notice.

The forest soon heard of Brother Alban's illness, for Dr. Gray Owl had a talkative wife.

"Did you hear," she said, "those unfortunate dwarfs have more trouble! The middle one, whom I always thought the least attractive—he has a sort of whiny scowl; you know what I mean—well, my dears, he's ill. Seriously ill too, Gray says. Heart. . . . Yes. . . . Well, I don't know *what* the others will do; he always looked after the housekeeping. Isn't it terrible? Just after losing that boy of theirs too. Well, they say troubles never come singly. Now don't repeat this; Gray told me in confidence . . ."

But, of course, there wasn't a soul in the forest who hadn't heard by the next day. Numerous little housewives shook their heads, murmured, "Dear, dear, the poor creatures," and baked little pies and cakes or made delicious soups, which they brought to the oak-tree house wrapped in checked napkins or packed into pretty little baskets.

"We thought you might find a use for this," they'd say timidly. Brother Ubald or Brother Botolph always received these gifts with such enthusiasm that the housewives were encouraged to give more.

Soon there was a regular path worn into the dwarfs' front lawn by the little feet of mercy. There was so much concern and interest taken in the progress of Brother Alban's health that Brother Ubald wrote out a bulletin every day, which Brother Botolph pinned on the oak tree. There usually were animals in front of it, studying it, and somehow this comforted the two brothers during the worst period, when it was still touch and go whether Brother Alban would pull through. Then came a long period of convalescence, in which Brother Alban had to be coaxed to eat.

"Do try some of Mamma Squirrel's delicious honeycake," Brother Botolph would murmur. "Or would you rather have the colts-foot jelly Mrs. Powderpuff sent—or a few spoonfuls of Mrs. Skunk-Phoo's chickory-noodle soup?"

Brother Alban would look up languidly and take the jelly, with an effort. Then he would relapse into a kind of coma.

The house was getting very dirty. The sink was stacked with unwashed dishes. Several families of mice had moved underneath it and were living entirely on the provisions that fell to the floor. Spiders also moved in and hung their apartments from the ceiling. Though they were clean and respectable, and made less noise than the mice, they were unpleasant neighbors, passing critical remarks on whatever the dwarfs happened to do.

"You'll never get that clean," they'd say, when they saw Brother Botolph struggling to mop the floor. "Clumsy idiot," they'd remark, when he dropped a plate. Brother Botolph thought of raising the rent on them; but then he realized that he wasn't up to the arguments that would ensue.

Perhaps of all the creatures in the forest, Mamma Squirrel had the softest heart, and she was therefore the most perturbed about the dwarfs' plight.

"I wish I were nearer them," she decided one day. "Why don't we move into the oak tree? Then I could keep an eye on them and lend a hand once in a while. It's not as if this house is so ideal, with those vulgar chipmunks right next door. One of the triplets said a rude word yesterday—copied from them, of course. The dwarfs live in a more genteel part of the forest, and there is a bit of open space around it on which the triplets can play games and that sort of thing. What do you say, Red?"

Mr. Squirrel was reading the *Gazette,* and only half attended to what his wife was saying. "As long as I don't have to do anything . . ." he murmured.

As if Mamma Squirrel would ever have asked for his help! She and Ross managed the whole move, of course. The triplets were too young to be anything but in the way, and Scarlet and Pinkie were each going steady and never available. When they weren't dreaming of marriage, they were curling their tails or off on a date.

Mr. Squirrel was very busy these days, as he had been offered a job on the *Gazette,* which he had accepted. He now divided his time between his memoirs and his journalistic work. His ambition was to write the editorials and influence public opinion. He felt eminently fitted for this. Unfortunately they were at present being written by Professor Hoot, who wrote dull passages such as:

In the case of juvenile delinquency we have another instance of the unbridled tendencies of our modern era. Far from taming the budding flower of our manhood, we cast adrift the stones of our future ship of state and continue to nurse the viper in our bosom for the paltry sum of a few moments' peace.

Mr. Squirrel felt that he could do better than that.

He had composed a song on Felix which had been printed in the *Gazette*.

RED SQUIRREL'S LAMENT

Our love is lost—what shall we do?
Uncurl our tails . . . alas . . . alack . . .
Felix—the name goes through and through
Our hearts. Come back, Felix, come back.

You were our friend, you shared our nuts,
Our nests were gladdened when you came,
Now all is gray—Felix, come back,
Without you, nothing is the same.

The dwarfs had wept when they read this. They didn't have the heart to object to having a squirrel family in their tree. When Mamma Squirrel came down to tidy their kitchen, they were even grateful.

Gradually Brother Alban began to feel better, and finally the day arrived when he was allowed to sit up in a chair. The others were very excited about it. Brother Ubald chose the softest armchair and made it more comfortable with his own pillows and blankets. Brother Botolph lit a roaring fire in the grate and had marshmallows handy for toasting.

Mamma Squirrel got wind of the event (she could follow

everything that went on by listening at the chimney) and
dressed up herself and the triplets to pay a visit. They carried gifts, of course—a special nut cake which it had taken
Mamma two days to bake, some acorn bread, and various
other delicacies.

"Now, take off your caps, dears," said Mamma Squirrel
proudly when they were admitted into the presence of the
invalid, who seemed to have disappeared entirely among
his cushions and blankets. "Say 'How do you do?' to dear
Uncle Alban. . . . The right paw, there's my good little men.
. . . I hope you don't mind my bringing them, Mr. Alban,
but they've been praying to the great Pan for you every day,

and they wanted so much to come. No, Carmine, don't touch those . . . they're marshmallows, honey, but not for you. Oh, Mr. Botolph, you're too kind, they shouldn't beg. Now, *one* then, Carmine. Yes, of course, Coral and Crimson may have one too, if Uncle Botolph permits it. . . . Now watch you don't mess. . . . Oh dear, all over your best suit. . . . Don't lick at it; put it into your mouth all at once and swallow. . . . Oh dear, she's choking . . ." Mamma Squirrel quickly held Coral upside down and saved the child's life. Then she caught Crimson before he fell into the fire, and prevented Carmine from playing with a knife. She didn't stay long, which was just as well, as poor Brother Alban still felt very weak.

However, he was on the mend and every day saw an improvement in his condition. The winter wasn't over yet before he was up and about, and very grateful for it.

"I never knew I'd enjoy washing dishes," he said, blinking watery eyes. He took longer to do things; he wasn't the dwarf he had been; but he felt happy. It seemed such a privilege to be alive.

Brother Ubald and Brother Botolph were happy too. It seemed to them such a privilege to have Brother Alban do the work again. And, true to their resolution, they helped him more. They dried the dishes after every meal, surprised him sometimes by making their own beds, and laid the table for him.

Brother Alban couldn't get over it. "Everyone is so kind

to me," he quavered. He still missed Felix very much, but it was a gentler ache than it had been in the beginning. He welcomed Felix's friends when they came to the door. Poor frozen forest children were allowed to warm themselves in his kitchen, and he always had an extra cup of soup for them. That seemed to bring Felix nearer, somehow.

Having the Squirrel family live in the same tree proved a comfort, as Mamma had hoped. She had a basket on a string, which she lowered to the dwarfs' front door, filled with little surprises. Brother Alban would return the compliment by placing a dish of his delicious mushroom goulash in the basket, or a special big pumpkin.

That way relations between the two households became friendlier and friendlier, and when Mamma Squirrel gave birth to twins early in the year the dwarfs were the first, after her, to see the babies. (Mr. Squirrel was out on an assignment for the *Gazette* at the time.)

The dwarfs gave her excellent advice on the feeding and bathing of infants. She called the twins Ruby and Rusty.

Soon it was quite a familiar sight to see one of the dwarfs dandling a squirrel baby on his lap, or feeding it, or changing its linen. This proved very lucky for Mamma too, for Ross had deserted her. He had discovered a very pretty little gray squirrel who lived in the ash tree beside the oak tree, and now he was always at her house, and Mamma scarcely ever saw him. She would have been very helpless and lonely without the dwarfs, but they had got so used to looking after Felix that it was a relief to them to take care of her.

And so the dark days passed, and the new spring with its sunshine and promise was just around the corner.

6. The Nectar Party

After so sad a winter, the spring seemed more of a miracle than ever. Never was there such stealthy growing and un-folding, such gentle surprises, such twittering and wooing and blooming and betrothing. Scarlet and Pinkie both got married. Their mother did not shed a tear.

"Why should I?" she said. "They're happy. They've both got good husbands who don't know what is in store for them."

Ross and little Griselda, his sweetheart, went for long climbs in the moonlight. They would have got married too if Ross had not been so solid and dependable. "I must first find a good job," he told her. "I want you to have a maid and all the comforts. You're not to slave and drudge, like my poor mamma. When I do things, I do them properly."

Griselda admired him very much for this, though she would rather have married right away. She wasn't sure she even *wanted* a maid. Wasn't it more fun to look after your own nest? However, already she realized that Ross knew best—which was just as well for her.

It was again the season of birth. As spring advanced, with more and more blossoms and babies, Brother Botolph began to feel worried about the way the young things were left to jump around, without supervision. In the old days he had only objected to the noise; now it worried him that the tiny creatures might get hurt.

"Look," he exclaimed one day, "Ruby almost broke her neck, falling out of the tree! Do you know what? I'll clear part of our yard, put in a swing and a sandbox, and then I'll tell the mothers to send their babies here, where they'll be safe." He had hardly thought of it when he was already sawing the wood for the fence. Soon he had made a beautiful playground. "If only I had had the wit to make one for Felix," he lamented, brushing a tear out of his eye.

The mothers of the forest were grateful. Every morning they brought their babies, and every evening they came to fetch them. Brother Botolph had even made a tiny pond for tadpoles, out of the way of ducks. He began to enjoy playing with the young folks, and could not understand why he had ever been cross with them.

Brother Ubald could not stay in the library while all this was going on. He took the storybooks Felix had liked best

and sat under a tree, reading aloud to whoever wanted to listen—and he never lacked an audience. Brother Alban would interrupt whatever was going on by sudden appearances, his arms full of surprises. Sometimes it was strings of popped corn, sometimes a huge dish of doughnuts, or baskets of peanuts, or cinnamon sticks to chew on, or toffee. Sometimes it was a bowl of soapy water and pipes, for blowing bubbles, or homemade paper trumpets, or colored hats. Whatever it was, it added to the general gaiety.

The dwarfs felt less and less lonely as they made more friends. They were always welcome at Mamma Squirrel's, where Mr. Squirrel, who had returned from his trip for the *Gazette,* had taken to reading aloud. He recited poetry or

read out his memoirs, and the dwarfs were full of admiration. "It's good to get the opinion of intelligent people, for a change," Mr. Squirrel told his wife.

When the Skunk-Phoos gave their annual nectar party, the dwarfs were invited, for the first time. After a certain amount of trepidation, they decided to accept.

Messrs. Ubald, Alban, and Botolph McOakum will be delighted to accept the kind invitation of Mr. and Mrs. Vincent Skunk-Phoo to a nectar party at "The Willows," Blueberry Avenue, King Oberon's Forest, at six P.M., July the twentieth inst.

They didn't know what "inst." meant, but it had been on the invitation, so they copied it. They copied RSVP also, only Mr. Squirrel saw their letter before they posted it and told them not to, for it only meant that they were to answer. The dwarfs felt rather annoyed about that.

"Of course we'd answer; where do they think we've learned our manners?" they grumbled.

Mr. Squirrel explained that it was just a custom. "It makes the invitation seem more important."

"Well, they could be important without insulting us," the dwarfs protested.

"Hardly," said Mr. Squirrel, who was used to society by now.

The dwarfs were in a great state of excitement about this party. They hadn't made a public appearance since their father's funeral, twenty years ago.

"What are we to wear?" they asked. Mr. Squirrel told them that everyone else would be putting on his best clothes. There would be a description of the general appearance of the most important guests. Naturally the dwarfs felt they were important, so this frightened them.

"I can't go in my overalls," Brother Botolph decided.

"Of course you can't," the others chorused. "We must look and see what we have in our trunk. What did we wear at the funeral?"

It turned out that there were three frock coats in the trunk which more or less fitted them. Mamma Squirrel said she'd press the coats. Brother Alban laundered three white shirts and polished three pairs of boots. They shampooed their beards the night before, and promised to look very smart.

"If only Felix could have seen us dressed up," they mourned. "He'd have been so proud."

Mamma Squirrel wasn't able to help them as much as they had hoped, for she had Mr. Squirrel's tie to fix, and his collar buttons to find, and his cuffs to fasten, besides putting on her own best suit and hat. Ross had promised to baby-sit for his mother. It was a cheap way of entertaining Griselda (he was going to read to her from the *Gazette*), and he was a frugal young man.

However, by fastening one another's cuffs, and brushing one another's backs, the dwarfs got dressed in proper fashion and set out, filled with anticipation. The wood was in a somnolent July mood. It had been a hot day, and midges danced between the dark, heavy leaves that already began to show yellow edges. They arrived early at the Skunk-Phoo mansion, set a little bit off the path and built under two willow trees. A maid—a sister of Miss Rosie Chipmunk, called Susie—in white cap and apron, opened the door for them. They expected to have their hands shaken in cordial welcome, but she merely looked over their heads and asked for their names. ("Just as if we weren't invited," Brother Alban muttered angrily.)

She then took their hats and coats and opened a door to the Skunk-Phoo living room, saying in a bored voice, "The Brothers McOakum."

Mr. Skunk-Phoo had on a simple suit—not half as elegant as their own, the dwarfs were pleased to observe. But Mrs. Skunk-Phoo had really pulled out all the stops. She was in a gold lamé gown, showing her whole back with its two white stripes. Her forelegs were covered, however, and she wore lace mitts on her paws. Her hair was smoothed away tight from her forehead, with a glistening lacquer on it. She wore big gold earrings and carried a long red cigarette holder with a cigarette in it, at which she puffed now and again in a manner which showed that it was really more trouble than it was worth.

"How do you *do?*" she said with sleepy exaltation when she saw the dwarfs. "Delighted you could come—simply *delighted.* Do make yourselves at home." Then she turned to Mrs. Powderpuff, who had just entered, trailing a scarf.

"How do you *do*?" she said in exactly the same tone. "Delighted you could come—simply *delighted*. Do make yourself at home."

The dwarfs didn't stop to listen to more. They mingled with the crowd, for a crowd was there already, at this early hour. There weren't enough chairs for people to sit down. The dwarfs were surprised at that: their mother had taught them that the first thing you offer a visitor is a chair. But here everyone was standing. Though it was a large, bare room, the atmosphere was getting smoky and it was hard to breathe. Several weasels, who had been hired for the evening, went around with trays bearing glasses of nectar. The dwarfs timidly took one each; as they sipped the nectar they noticed that it had a rather stinging taste. They stood shyly together, with their backs to the wall. They hadn't realized how many people they did not know.

At last they caught sight of a familiar face: it was Archibald, in a white sailor suit. "Hullo," they said, but Archibald merely gave them a nod and went on. His interest was in the food, he had his eye on various little canapés and small rolls that were being served, and managed to intercept several dishes, which never reached their destination.

"I don't know why we were invited," whispered Brother Ubald to Brother Alban. "No one pays the slightest attention to us; nobody seems to want to talk to us. It is more comfortable at home, where we can sit down. Let's leave."

"Wait a minute—the Squirrels have just arrived; let's say hello to them first," proposed Brother Alban. They had taken so much trouble dressing, it seemed a pity to go before anyone had had a chance to admire them. Mr. Squirrel had already caught sight of them and was working his way to them through the crowd. He seemed to know everybody; there were cries of, "Hi, Red, how's the memoirs? . . . Write me up, please! . . . I've got a piece of news for you, Red. . . . Meet my niece, Red, she has been longing to be introduced to you; she so much admired your poem in the *Gazette*. . . . Red, listen to this one, you'll die laughing . . ." and that sort of thing. Red smiled, sparkled, twinkled, but steadily worked his way to the dwarfs.

"Ooph!" he sighed when he reached them. "Hasn't anyone introduced you to anyone, the way you three are standing there as if you were up for auction? . . . Come along with me, then, and I'll show you the life of the forest. The great thing about nectar parties is that you can do what you like. It's no use being modest, you know; that's out of fashion now. People will think as much of you as you think yourself. See that woodchuck over there? He is a common enough fellow, hasn't anything to say for himself, but he studied the fashion journals and made himself look so smart that he is invited to the best parties. He knows he is not interesting, so he never says a word, but looks through his monocle and makes others feel inferior. Here is an amusing creature, though—she is our fashion editor, and she may put you in the paper, if you like. Miss Pigeon, may I introduce you to the Brothers McOakum?"

"Oh, *dwarfs*," said Miss Pigeon with a delighted giggle. "I adore dwarfs! *Do* tell me *all* about yourselves. It's hot, isn't it?—hotter than usual at this time of the year. Have you played any golf lately? . . . Oh, you never do. . . . No, of course, one can overdo sports. . . . Yes, I entirely agree with you; it is all so superficial. You dwarfs are awfully learned, I hear. My father used to know your father, I believe. . . . Didn't you write something. . . . Oh, I see; no, perhaps it was somebody else I was thinking of. Oh, there is Mrs. Pheasant—do excuse me; I promised . . ." Miss Pigeon had fluttered off, and Mr. Squirrel was nowhere to be seen either. The dwarfs were again left to themselves.

"Let's go home," Brother Ubald proposed, but just at that moment the waiters came round with a dish of delicious cream buns, and the dwarfs couldn't resist taking one each. They felt weak from standing. Unfortunately, there was more cream in the buns than they had anticipated. It spouted up their noses, lodged in their beards, and spread over their cheeks. It was a funny sight, and people in the neighborhood began to giggle. The dwarfs tried frantically to lick up the superfluous cream; their tongues, however, did not stretch far enough, and the result was worse. It was exactly as if they'd been soaped up for a shave. Conscious of mocking glances aimed at them from all directions, they hauled forth their handkerchiefs and wiped one another's faces.

"What antediluvian characters," they heard a fashionable wood hen say. "Where did dear Vincent dig *them* up?"

"They are probably here for comic relief," her partner drawled.

The dwarfs were deeply hurt. They had been so long away from society that they had forgotten what it feels like to be criticized.

"Let's go," they whispered, quickly pocketing their sticky handkerchiefs. But now that they wanted to slip away unnoticed they seemed to meet everyone they knew.

"Ah, the dwarfs!" cried Professor Hoot. "Dear Ubald, may I introduce you to my wife? . . . Honey, here are the dwarfs you've heard so much about. Ubald is an extremely learned man."

"How do you do—pleased to meet you. Ah! There's Mr. Fox. Mr. Fox, have you met our dwarfs? This is their first appearance after Brother Alban's illness," said Mrs. Hoot.

"I have been longing to meet you," the fox uttered huskily, with a deep bow and a glare through his lorgnettes. "I have heard so much of the good you have done in the forest lately, looking after our underprivileged children. Oh, Miss Badger, come and meet the dwarfs. We were talking of them only the other day, weren't we, and praising the decline of juvenile delinquency since they started their charitable work."

"Indeed, Mr. Oakum, I *did* long to meet you. How delightful of you to think of those nurseries. It's made *all* the difference, I *assure* you—"

"How did you *think* of it?" twittered a Miss Nightingale, a fashionable opera singer who was languishing on the arm of an admirer. "I should *love* to amuse the kiddies if I did not have such a delicate constitution, but one gets such headaches from them, doesn't one?"

"How do you find *time* for it all!" exclaimed a snail, fanning herself.

"It's a gift," sighed sentimental Miss Dove.

The dwarfs were embarrassed. They had been so long

away from society that they had forgotten what it feels like to be praised.

"I think we'll have to be going," they muttered, nervously wiping their hands on their trousers.

But now Mamma Squirrel had caught sight of them, with a delighted squeal. Mr. Squirrel was such a celebrity that he had long ago deserted her, and she had stood about awkwardly without a soul to talk to and been pushed around by gesticulating neighbors. The dwarfs had to chat with her for a while, and fetch her some cakes (she didn't drink the nectar, she said). They warned her seriously against the cream buns, and one look at Mrs. Powderpuff, who was, at that moment, immersed in one without hope of deliverance (to the solid amusement of all around her), convinced Mamma Squirrel that they were to be avoided at all costs.

"I've never been to a party like this before," she told the dwarfs in a loud voice. "Red seems to enjoy them, but I don't think they're much fun, do you? I'd rather have tea with a friend, where I can sit down and exchange news. I can't hear myself here, let alone anyone else."

"Hush," said the dwarfs, looking around to see if the hostess had noticed.

"It's all very stylish, though; I can see that," Mamma Squirrel went on. "Look at the mimsy-pimsy faces. It's all *dear* so-and-so, and *dear* so-and-so, and when they move away you hear all the bad about them. Do you think they'd miss me if I left?"

"Red might," Brother Botolph told her.

"Not at all," said Mamma. "I think I'll go home."

"We're going too," the dwarfs told her. "Where are Mr. and Mrs. Skunk-Phoo, so we can say good-by?"

But Mr. and Mrs. Skunk-Phoo had retired upstairs, where they were lying on their beds, reading novels and eating chocolates. They did not enjoy their own parties. So the dwarfs and Mamma Squirrel left without saying good-by.

After this taste of society the dwarfs decided they would stay at home in the future. One can overdo it, they felt. They had nice neighbors, and that was enough.

Even the write-up in the *Gazette* didn't reconcile them to nectar parties. All it said about them was: "The Brothers McOakum, looking magnificent in real antique suits, were present."

They were even a little worried about the description. "It doesn't *sound* right," they told Mamma Squirrel. "I know an antique clock is a good thing, or an antique table —but an antique suit—"

"*I* should worry," said Mamma Squirrel, who was happily pottering about in her old housecoat and slippers. "I bet you they can't think of enough new words to describe clothes."

That sounded reasonable, and the dwarfs forgot about it. All that oppressed them now was how to return hospitality. "We can't give a nectar party," they decided. "We haven't the room."

Besides, they were too busy. Brother Alban hadn't his full strength yet, and with all the extra work they had undertaken, the dwarfs had little free time. But whatever they did flourished in a way it hadn't before. Brother Botolph's garden was a joy to behold. The same animals who used to pester him now helped him, out of gratitude for his kindness—and also because they liked gardening. Never had his cucumbers been so fat, his corn so high, his tomatoes so red, his melons so sweet. He gave away a lot and yet kept more than he had ever had.

Mamma Squirrel was especially glad of his gifts, for she

now had three households to feed. Little as she had seen of Scarlet and Pinkie before they were married, now they were always under foot. They borrowed her milk, her bread, her vegetables (and never paid back, of course). They used her bobbypins, her scissors, her sewing materials. They walked off with her frying pans, her cookbooks, her dish towels.

"Aren't your husbands capable of supporting you?" Mr. Squirrel would remark angrily when he found out.

"Oh yes," they drawled, "but it's so much easier to come to dear Mamma."

"I'll 'dear mamma' you!" cried Mr. Squirrel, and bit them. That taught them a lesson. It was three days before they appeared again.

The dwarfs felt sorry for Mamma Squirrel. "All the same," they decided, "it's her own fault. She is too kind. She has no discipline. Remember how we used to punish Felix? He'd never have behaved like that." And they'd climb up on their little ladder to Mamma Squirrel's house to tell her at least to whip the little ones before it was too late. They feared, though, that Mamma Squirrel was incorrigible. If only Mr. Squirrel had been there oftener— But he was getting more and more assignments from the *Gazette* to different parts of the forest and becoming a really famous reporter.

Meanwhile the summer was dying, and again the leaves were beginning to fall.

7. Felix Returns

October had come round again. The forest children in Brother Botolph's playground began to whisper the word "Halloween." The dwarfs looked at one another and burst out laughing.

"What a silly quarrel," said Brother Alban, with a chuckle.

"Why shouldn't the children have some fun?" queried Brother Botolph.

"What was the fuss *about*?" Brother Ubald wanted to know.

"We are going to give a party this time," Brother Botolph announced to his playground children. "You must all help prepare for it. We'll hollow out our biggest pumpkin and

121

scare the whole forest with it. We'll make whistles and toot-ers and masks. We'll put candles inside jack-o'-lanterns, and we'll invite all the glowworms and fireflies we know."

The young creatures cried "Hurray!" and ran home to tell the news. Soon the whole forest was buzzing with ex-citement. The dwarfs were going to give a party—the first one in a hundred years!

Presently invitations were sent out.

The Brothers McOakum request the pleasure of your com-pany at a garden party to be held at their residence: Oaklands, Cloverplace, King Oberon's Forest, at 8 P.M. on October thirty-first inst. Fancy Dress optional. RSVP.

They had debated a while about "RSVP," having resented this on their own invitation; but after discussing it with Mr. Squirrel, they decided to put it in.

"You will want to know how much food you'll need," he pointed out. "And a lot of the people you have invited are ignorant and unable to hold a pen well. They may have to go to Professor Hoot to have their answers written for them, which will mean they'll have to pay him. If you won't put in 'RSVP' they'll never do it; you have no idea how rude some people are." Mr. Squirrel was becoming so much the man of the world that his wife marveled at it and counted herself luckier than ever.

Soon acceptances came pouring in—elegant, gilt-edged stationery from Mrs. Skunk-Phoo; a dirty little scrawl from

Mrs. Powderpuff; and a lot of identical messages written in the beautiful script of Professor Hoot.

The three dwarfs worked hard for the remaining weeks of October. It amazed them how much work there is to giving a party, and there were moments when they sat together at their table as of old, groaning that they wished they had never started the thing. But then they would remember the bright faces of their forest children and take heart again.

It was an exceptionally beautiful fall. There were so many toadstools that there was no need to worry about seats, though the dwarfs made some wooden benches for bigger animals. They also made a little wooden stage, for there was to be a performance. Mr. Squirrel had written a play for the forest children, and the fairy ballet was to come and dance. Besides, the dwarfs hoped to perform as conjurers. Mamma Squirrel had made them lovely black magician's cloaks with glittering gold stars, which suited them to perfection.

Mr. Squirrel insisted on going as a knight and had made some sort of costume out of silver paper, but it was not very successful. The helmet just looked like a lot of silver paper crushed together. He had stolen a feather from Mrs. Pheasant to stick on it, but that did not really help. Mrs. Squirrel secretly thought it looked silly, though she did not like to tell him so. Ross said it. Ross said, "For goodness' sake, Pa, don't wear that. What will Griselda think?"

"What's wrong with it?" Mr. Squirrel wanted to know, huffily.

"It doesn't look like anything, except a Christmas tree."

"It's a perfectly good helmet," insisted Mr. Squirrel. But privately he tried to give it a better shape. Sometimes it looked like a teapot and sometimes like a saucepan, but never like a helmet.

"I've got to wear *something*," he grumbled. At the last moment he grew so discouraged that he said he wasn't going to the party at all and retired to bed with all his clothes on. Mamma Squirrel told the children to be quiet and got him out again by assuring him that the helmet looked magnificent.

Luckily All Hallow's Eve turned out to be fine—sunny, and not too cold. The dwarfs worked hard to get last-minute jobs done. Brother Alban baked delicious cakes and cookies for the buffet supper; Brother Ubald went over the words of the play with the actors; Brother Botolph and his helpers decorated the yard.

At the appointed time the visitors arrived. The dwarfs received them in their lovely magicians' costumes. Their garden looked as pretty as could be, with garlands of glow-worms obligingly suspended from tree to tree and fireflies flitting in formation, making luminous patterns in the air. (It was rather late in the season for them, and they had to be paid overtime. They all had little fur wraps which they put on between their acts.) There were lighted jack-o'-

lanterns, and a great big pumpkin grinning from ear to ear.

Scarlet and Pinkie had consented to look after the cloak-room, which was a tent under a dogwood tree. They looked very pretty, dressed up as shepherdesses, and enjoyed themselves examining the various coats and hats and costumes. It has to be admitted that they were a little fresh and said to Mrs. Skunk-Phoo, who came wrapped in a mink cloak, which covered the dazzling costume of an Arabian princess, "Toss me your pelt, toots." Luckily she didn't hear this, because of the general noise.

There were some magnificent costumes. Mr. Skunk-Phoo, when divested of coat and hat, stood revealed as an enormous perfume bottle, with loud advertisements on the

labels of the latest scent his company had produced. He made a good foil for the Arabian princess, who was sprinkled heavily with the same perfume and had tiny little sample bottles hanging from wrist and ankles. As a matter of fact, Mr. Skunk-Phoo had wanted his wife to go as the bottle. He wasn't keen on dressing up. But his wife had refused. She said it was not a costume likely to flatter her figure. Mr. Skunk-Phoo had been so enamored of the idea of getting a little free advertisement that he had overcome his reluctance to don the costume himself. But he secretly felt that his wife had let him down, and was rather grumpy in consequence.

Professor Hoot arrived dressed as a Spanish don, with a black wig, a velvet hat and drooping white feather. Mr. Soames Turtle had fixed a whole Noah's ark on his back, filled with snails, ants, and crickets, which kept falling out and having to be waited for to climb on again, thus impeding Mr. Turtle's already slow and ponderous advance. However, it was worth it, for there was general applause when he finally arrived at the party. The two Miss Doves came as cupids, with sweet little gold-paper bows and arrows. Mrs. Powderpuff had made herself up as Cinderella, but she had sewn her crepe-paper dress so carelessly that she not only lost her shoe but her whole costume before the evening was out. There was a crowd of young forest children in the usual disguises of clowns, gypsies, and Spanish dancers.

Soon the lantern lights shone on a merry throng who were milling around and helping themselves to the lemonade, which was served by the five youngest squirrels, dressed prettily like flowers. The dwarfs walked around beaming at everyone. A cricket band began to play on a special podium, near the stage, and some young people began to dance. Mr. Squirrel—always the center of any fun—invited a shy young mole to do a foxtrot with him. She blinked behind her glasses and said she could not dance, so he went and did a bunny-hop with Sympathy Powderpuff instead.

Ross and Griselda were already dancing, and Scarlet and Pinkie got so excited that their husbands thought it best for them to go home. As a result the cloakroom was left to look after itself, and for days afterward the dwarfs had people knocking at the door, asking for missing scarfs, gloves, and hats.

Archibald had become a fashionable youngster. He'd been to dancing school and wore white gloves. He was waltzing away with his cousin, Annie Skunk, a girl of no importance, but pretty. His mother looked on tolerantly. She already had his bride picked out for him, and meanwhile he could amuse himself as he liked.

"Doesn't Mr. Squirrel look ridiculous with that silver-paper wig on?" she said to her husband. "What's he supposed to represent—a judge?"

"Where, my dear?" asked Mr. Skunk-Phoo, who was not observant. "Oh, there? Oh, is that a wig? I thought it was a turban and that he was supposed to be one of those Eastern fellows."

Luckily Mr. Squirrel did not hear these remarks, or it would have spoiled the evening for him. He was trying to find out from his partner what she thought of his costume, but as she had a missing tooth it was hard to understand her answers. This was just as well, as she had been trying to tell him she thought him a "thplendid under-thea thwimmer."

"I think all the guests have arrived by now, and the little ones are getting impatient. We'd better put on our play," Brother Botolph told his brothers. They were rather anxious to have it over with, as they were suffering from stage fright. The orchestra was told to stop playing. One of the forest children blew on his horn, and Brother Ubald climbed on the stage to deliver his opening speech.

"Ladies and gentlemen," he said in a trembling voice, glancing down at a paper he had in his hand. Goodness, he had it upside down! There was a pause while he turned it around and cleared his throat. "Ladies and gentlemen—" He peered hard at the writing, but it was too small. He had not counted on the dim light. "Ladies and gentlemen—Oh, bother it, I can't read this, I just wanted to tell you you're all very welcome and we hope you'll enjoy yourselves; we've got up a little performance we hope you'll like and—I guess that's about all. I had a lovely speech . . . but it can't be helped." There was a great cheering after this. Everyone felt secretly relieved to have been spared the speech.

Mr. Squirrel's play was no great thing, just an occasion for the forest offspring to show off pretty costumes, recite some poetry, and go through a few dancing steps. It was a success, however, for each parent melted as his own child came on and never bothered to look at the others. The best part was, of course, when the youngest came on—Mrs. Powderpuff's week-old baby, three young mice, and a wee chipmunk. They were adorable, dressed in white ballet costumes and each of them totteringly trying to balance on one leg. There were "ooohs" and "aaahs" from the audience.

"Aren't they cute? Look at that wee Andy Chipmunk—he isn't even *listening* to the music. Did you see him peering at his mother through his paws? Oh, and Isolde Powderpuff —the rogue—she isn't even *trying*. She is just sitting down, picking her wreath to pieces. Aren't babies sweet!"

The other children felt a little hurt, because they had really practiced, and the failure of the babies seemed to get more applause than their own successes, but Brother Botolph consoled them. "Everybody knows you're better," he said. "They are praising the little ones out of pity." That made sense to them.

The next item was to be the fairy ballet. But the fairy prima ballerina had not arrived yet. Agitated hobgoblins

ran to the dwarfs, bearing pink messages from the fairies, who sat huddled in the cloakroom, which was also the dressing room for the performers. They didn't care to mix with the audience, feeling themselves above mere animals and dwarfs. The pink messages conveyed the news in staccato sentences that until Milady Mirafleur, First Fairy, had arrived, there would be no dancing.

The dwarfs felt worried. They had more or less counted on the fairies to carry off the brunt of the entertainment. The play had been slight and, though they planned to do some conjuring tricks themselves which they hoped would come off, they felt that there should be more solid entertainment first. And the fairy ballet was famous—no one who has not seen it can imagine the grace and subtlety and splendor of fairies dancing.

They decided, therefore, to wait for Milady Mirafleur,

telling the audience that there would be a short interval before the next act. They waited in vain. Milady Mirafleur was at that moment sailing off on a magic carpet with Queen Titania's page. She was tired of being a ballerina, and preferred wedded life in a palace. No doubt she was right, but she should not have forgotten her promise to the dwarfs, and she might at least have let the other fairies in the ballet know.

Meanwhile the guests were getting restive. They felt that the interval was too long. They began to whistle and giggle and make noises. The forest children who had acted in the play were overexcited and began to run around, asking for "tricks or treats," which embarrassed the other guests. The atmosphere became unpleasant. Mrs. Powderpuff let her ear flop into the face of a rather narrow-minded, elderly mole, who objected in an ill-tempered way. Mrs. Powderpuff defended herself shrilly. Others joined in the argument and made tactless remarks that ruffled feelings further. The poor dwarfs were frantic. What was happening to their party? They went to the cloakroom and pleaded with the fairies to come on, anyway, but the fairies were indignant at the very suggestion; they said they had their professional honor to consider. In fact, they were so annoyed, they put on their wraps and left in a huff, the hobgoblins trotting after them and carrying their parcels.

"Well, we'll have to do our conjuring act and hope for the best," said Brother Botolph. "We can't let the guests wait any longer; they're getting noisier and noisier. Oh, why did we let ourselves in for this!" And he mopped his brow. He felt nervous. The audience was less friendly than before.

There was only slight applause when Brother Botolph came onto the stage for the first trick. There were murmurs of, "This had better be good, after all that waiting," which disconcerted him. He blushed timidly and spread out a handkerchief. "Watch," he said in a croaky voice. "Now you see it—and now you don't." He spread out miraculously empty hands, but unfortunately the handkerchief was hanging out of one of his sleeves. There was loud laughter, especially from the young folk, who pointed out the mistake with glee. Brother Botolph hastily stuffed the handkerchief up his sleeve, but it was too late.

He coughed. "Trick Number Two," he announced hurriedly.

Now Brother Alban appeared with a pack of cards. He shuffled it and made Brother Botolph select one. Brother Botolph picked one out and held it up so that the audience could see it—but not Brother Alban. It was the queen of hearts.

"Put it back," said Brother Alban, and he shuffled the pack again. "Here it is!" he cried, holding up a card. There was an explosion of laughter. It was the three of spades. Brother Alban had tears in his eyes. What had gone wrong? The trick had succeeded perfectly the day before!

Several young hares and badgers at the back of the audience got up and left. "Kid stuff," they muttered. "Why waste our time?"

Mr. Skunk-Phoo looked impatiently at his gold watch.

"We have another trick," Brother Botolph announced desperately. This time Brother Ubald appeared on the stage, carrying a tall hat. They had rented the hat from a witch who sold conjuring tricks. It had a double compartment in the top. Brother Ubald turned it upside down.

"Abracadabra," he said. "We shall now witness a marvelous piece of magic. I shall break an egg in this tall hat and watch what happens!" There was an expectant sigh from the audience as the dwarfs broke an egg into the glossy black hat. Brother Botolph plunged in his hand to pull out the artificial paper chicken hidden in its false top. Instead his hand encountered only sticky egg stuff, and, looking closely, he saw the name Vincent Skunk-Phoo sewn on the hatband. Brother Ubald had brought the wrong hat!

The dwarfs exchanged anguished looks. What to do now? Already the audience was beginning to hiss. Oh, what to do? They were lost! Mr. Skunk-Phoo would be very angry; the party was spoiled. But suddenly they heard, "Cack, cack, cackle!" and a real little live hen crawled out of the hat, spread its wings, and flew away.

The audience began to clap furiously, but they were not more surprised than the dwarfs. What had happened? Had they suddenly become true magicians? They looked into the

hat, and saw a beautiful bouquet of flowers in it. Brother
Alban lifted it out with trembling hands.

"To Mrs. Skunk-Phoo," it said on a label, in exquisitely
fine handwriting. He tossed it to her, amid "oohs" and
"aahs" from the audience. Next there was a silver watch in
the hat, marked "For Archibald." The dwarfs told Archibald to come and fetch it, which he did, amid deafening
applause.

The dwarfs were more and more amazed. They pulled
one thing after another out of Mr. Skunk-Phoo's hat. There
was a silk shawl for Mamma Squirrel, a small vacuum
cleaner for Mrs. Powderpuff, a fountain pen for Professor
Hoot, balloons for the children—in fact, no one was forgotten—and at last, most splendid of all, there was a plumed
silver helmet for Mr. Squirrel.

That was the final gift. The hat was empty and immaculate. Not a trace of egg remained. Brother Botolph handed it politely to Mr. Skunk-Phoo, apologizing for having borrowed it. There were roars and cheers and clappings. The whole atmosphere had changed. People whispered how amazingly clever the dwarfs were, and how generous— what a nice idea to give everyone a present, and in such an original way too—they couldn't *imagine* how it was done!

Indeed, neither could the dwarfs. They still felt dazed as they announced that supper would be served.

"Do you know," whispered Brother Ubald to Brother Botolph, while the guests were trooping to the long tables on which Brother Alban, helped by Mamma Squirrel, was hurriedly placing food, "Do you know, I think I recognize the handwriting on the labels. It's much better than it used to be, but Felix always did have difficulty making a proper 'r.' "

"You mean—"

"It's Felix, I'm certain. He is somewhere near and he helped us out when he saw that the party was going to be a failure."

"But—it was magic."

"We don't know what happened to Felix. He may be able to do magic now," said Brother Ubald. "I feel, somehow, that he is very close."

"Don't tell Brother Alban," whispered Brother Botolph. "He'd get too excited."

Brother Alban at that moment was too busy to be told anything. He was carrying big plates of doughnuts, enormous cakes, plates with sandwiches, nuts, and fruit, and serving them to the guests, who were eating away with passionate pleasure. They had got very hungry during the performance.

Each guest had his own way of eating. Mr. and Mrs. Skunk-Phoo ate with dignity, holding little plates under their chins and using forks even for cupcakes. The squirrel children ran to the table, chose something, and ran back to hide while they were eating it. Archibald sat down and steadily devoured everything within reach. Mrs. Powderpuff talked and ate at the same time, which caused her to choke frequently.

Mr. Squirrel, resplendent in his new helmet, which suited him to perfection, now raised his glass and stood up. "I propose a vote of thanks to our hosts!" he said. "Seldom have we attended a more gay and generous party. The dwarfs have outdone themselves. Here's to them!"

"Hurray, hurray!" cried the guests. Someone began to sing, "For they are jolly good fellows." There was a tumult of noise, during which the good dwarfs wept quietly, not only because they were touched by the kindness of their guests, but also because they felt that the party was a year too late. If only they'd had it last year, Felix might still be with them now. And how he'd have enjoyed it!

And then, gradually, the noise died down, and the moon,

till now hardly visible in the sky, seemed to grow brighter and stronger and shed a silver light over the festive table. The guests stopped eating and looked up in wonder. Stronger and stronger waxed the silver light, until the leaves above their heads were bathed in it and seemed to sprout tinsel halos. The dark sky in between became luminous and quivered.

Was this another trick of the dwarfs? But they seemed as astonished as the rest. Now a bright beam shot through the trees from an unknown, hidden source of light. It was a dazzling beam of many colors, prettier than any fireworks. There were sighs of ecstasy from the guests. They all held their breath, and looked. The beam grew broader and thinner and seemed to fan out as it reached the ground. And suddenly, out of it, emerged a splendid knight on a winged milk-white horse that stamped its gold hoofs and champed a little gold bit. The knight was young and slender, clad in silver armor, with a shiny helmet on his fair waving curls. It was only when he smiled that they were able to recognize him.

"Felix!" they cried. "Felix! Felix!"

"Felix," sobbed the dwarfs, hurriedly rising from the table. The silver light slowly ebbed, and Felix became more and more recognizable as the lantern light took over, casting shadows and revealing his solidity.

"Yes, it's me," he said simply, dismounting from his horse and throwing the reins over a branch. The forest children,

who were more interested in the horse than in Felix, fed it sugar lumps and it soon could be heard crunching them contentedly.

The older guests were in a sort of stupor, watching the reunion of Felix and his foster parents with awe. Mrs. Powderpuff was so overcome that Ross had to throw a glass of lemonade over her to revive her. Such was the splendor of Felix that the dwarfs bowed before him, until he himself embraced them, telling them not to be foolish.

"But, Felix—what happened to you?" stammered Brother Botolph, who was the first to find himself able to speak.

"Give me some of those delicious pies, and a glass of lemonade, and I'll tell you," said Felix.

Immediately there was a bustle of activity as Mamma Squirrel, her children, the dwarfs, and many other guests all vied with one another to offer him a chair, a plate, food, and drink and a napkin. After he was happily seated and duly refreshed (quite unconscious of the spectacle he provided), he began to talk, and even the crickets stopped chirping to listen to him.

He began by telling of his first encounter with the king and of the gift of the gold key. The dwarfs had not heard this before.

"I kept thinking about it," Felix continued. "I wanted very much to be one of the king's knights, but I was also afraid of the dragon. Then, on Halloween night last year,

I was alone in my room, thinking about that dragon. I could almost smell him. And suddenly I wanted to crush him more than I wanted anything in the world. I wanted to be beside the king, to fight with him. I longed and longed for it, and then a queer light filled my room. It shone like a beam, and in the middle of the beam was a tunnel, and at the end of the tunnel was the door of the king's palace. All I had to do was get up and go there and unlock the door. The king was waiting for me. I—I can't tell about that—"

Felix faltered and blushed. His eyes were wet. No one spoke. After a while Felix continued. "The king was in trouble. You do not know, here in the forest, the troubles of your king. That dragon wants to grab this whole forest for his very own. If he got it he would take away its light, and it would be night and winter forever, and there'd be no friendship left. The king has to fight him all the time. Several times he thought he had killed him, but he appeared again at another side of the forest. The king was running out of knights, and he asked me if I would be one, and I said 'Yes, oh yes.' "

Felix stopped for a moment, casting down his eyes and crumbling a bun. Then he took a deep breath and went on. "I went to a school where I learned to fight dragons. I also learned a little magic. (Here he winked at the dwarfs.) Now I have been knighted, I have my gold spurs, and I am called Sir Felix. I am free to go where I like. I shall visit you all often; I won't forget you. Nor will the king, of course.

He sends you all his greetings, and I have something special for my papas."

Felix got up and went to his horse, who was having a wonderful time being petted, and out of his saddlebag he fetched a scroll. Unrolling it, he read out what was written on it. It was a formal declaration, conferring the order of the Knights of Oberon on the three dwarfs, for their labors in bringing up Sir Felix. It was signed by the king himself. While the dwarfs were speechlessly fingering the document in turns, their eyes filled with tears, Felix hung a scarlet ribbon with a gold medal around the neck of each of them.

Now the silence of attention that had reigned while Felix spoke was shattered by an explosion of joy and congratulations from the animals. The dwarfs did not know what to say. They were overwhelmed. Mr. Skunk-Phoo said it instead. He got up, tapped his glass, settled his monocle more firmly in his eye, and, forgetting his ridiculous costume, launched into a formal speech of thanks. Clearing his throat, he began, "Sir Felix, ladies and gentlemen of the forest. Words fail me on this momentous occasion. Little did we think that the orphan who lived among us would one day become the right hand of King Oberon. But those of us who knew him well in his childhood are not really surprised." He glanced benignly at Sir Felix. "I for one, am not."

He waited for the applause that followed this statement, and continued. "The ways of destiny are inscrutable. Who can say whether other circumstances might not have brought any one of us to the notice of King Oberon? Therefore we forest people, rejoicing at the honor conferred on the dwarfs, must regret the turn of fate"—here a note of bitterness crept into his voice—"which brought Felix to the home of the dwarfs rather than to any one of ours. This honor which is conferred on the dwarfs tonight, is, in a sense, shared by all the forest people, who were by fortune's whim deprived of the privilege of opening their humble abodes to so illustrious a guest. Nevertheless we, as friends of the dwarfs, do not begrudge them their well-deserved honor, and we would ask Sir Felix to convey to His Majesty the warm sentiments of affection and loyalty with which this reward fills us. At the same time we hope he will not fail to inform King Oberon of the attachment, to him, of each and every one in this forest. I therefore venture to hope that this distinction may not be the last one to be conferred on one of his forest people."

Amidst deafening applause Mr. Skunk-Phoo sat down.

" 'Turn of fate,' 'fortune's whim,' my eye!" cried Mr. Squirrel indignantly, jumping up so suddenly that his much-prized new helmet slid over one ear. "I never heard such bunk in all my life. I may not be an orator, as Mr. Skunk-Phoo is, but I know the truth when I see it. Does Mr. Skunk-Phoo ask us to believe that he was anxious to adopt orphans? We all know he has only one child; we know he has plenty of goods; we know he has a large house; and we know that there are hundreds of orphans in this forest. As a not-too-perfect father of a large family I can appreciate fully what it must have cost the dwarfs—three bachelors unversed in child care—to accept the charge of a newborn baby. Let's be honest and acknowledge that the forest deserves no credit at all. It was the dwarfs who had the troubles and the sorrows and who should now have the honor. May I add, Sir Felix," the squirrel continued, humbly turning toward the knight, "that I should very much like to offer my services to the king—in whatever capacity—" Here emotion overcame him, and he sat down in confusion.

There was some applause, though Mrs. Skunk-Phoo was heard to hiss "Upstart," and to make signs to her husband that she wanted to leave. Her husband, however, had just discovered that his costume was coming apart and was too busy trying to fix it to pay attention to his wife.

Brother Botolph and Brother Alban had been nudging Brother Ubald to get up and speak. Brother Ubald was slow to respond, but when an awkward silence seemed to settle over the table, he shyly rose.

"Thank you all very much," he said in a quivering voice. "Thank you. We are not thinking of the honor at all—though we are grateful, of course. All we feel is that our boy is back, that he is alive and has grown into a splendid knight. That is what matters. Thank you." And he sat down again.

This time the applause was so loud and long that it

stopped only when Sir Felix arose in his turn. "I shall have to say good-by now," he said. "I hope to be back soon and often, but now I must return to the king. I shall tell him of your loyalty." Turning to Mr. Squirrel, he added with a smile, "I know that you would like to fight by my side. But you have other duties at present. However, hold yourself ready; the king may want you some time. Loyal hearts are what he needs most. Now, my dear friends, I must go. Thank you for all your kindness. Till we meet again."

Felix waved his hand at the guests, embraced the dwarfs, and mounted his horse. The horse spread its broad white wings, moving them swiftly until they seemed to make a halo of silver light around horse and rider. This halo grew brighter and denser, until it looked like a soap bubble, and lightly floated off into the sky, where it could be seen no more.

The dwarfs had stared after it, and now gazed at their guests in a bewildered way. They fiddled with their medals.

"The poor creatures are overcome—let's leave them in peace," murmured Mamma Squirrel, coaxing the guests toward the cloakroom. Most of them departed willingly; they were growing sleepy and there was so much to think over. But Mrs. Powderpuff kept walking about the lawn, searching for various missing parts of her costume, while Mrs. Skunk-Phoo insisted on taking formal leave of the dwarfs. She first tried to find Archibald, to make him do the same, but Archibald had gone off to bring Annie home.

Mr. Skunk-Phoo had also vanished. (He was trying to find his topcoat among a jumble of clothes in the cloakroom, and, rather than go home as a perfume bottle, he was forced to put on someone else's topcoat in the end.)

So it was only Mrs. Skunk-Phoo who finally went up to the dwarfs, shook hands with them, and thanked them for the party. "We've had a wonderful time," she told them. "You went to so much trouble. If I can ever do anything for you, just let me know. We'd very much like you to come to dinner one night; perhaps you can persuade Sir Felix to come too. That will give you a change of company. You have been too good-natured, letting those common squirrels move into your tree. They must be a trial to you—such a rowdy family . . ."

The dwarfs murmured something. They felt exhausted and were grateful that most of the guests tactfully left without formalities. They knew that their party had been a success, thanks to Felix, and were anxious to sit down and rest and talk things over.

"Go on in," Mamma Squirrel told them, when she saw them waiting politely while Mrs. Powderpuff collected her belongings. "I'll attend to her. You must be tired out."

Gratefully the dwarfs withdrew into their little house. They were carrying a lantern, which they put on the table. Brother Alban looked pale. Brother Botolph made him sit in the easiest chair, with his feet up.

"But I want to get you your hot-water bottles," he said.

"Not at all; don't you stir," Brother Botolph told him. "It's been much too exciting a day for you, and we can't have you ill again. Brother Ubald and I shall look after everything."

"It is so good of you," murmured Brother Alban. "I confess I am a bit faint. I thought my heart would stop for joy when I recognized Felix. *Oh,* I am so happy, so grateful." He leaned back in his chair with a look of peace on his face. His brothers took off his shoes and fetched his slippers. They felt anxious about him.

"I'll never forget our conjuring party." Brother Alban chuckled. "Do you remember the moment we discovered that Brother Ubald had brought the wrong hat?"

"There was such a mess in the cloakroom," explained Brother Ubald sheepishly. "I'd forgotten that Mr. Skunk-Phoo wears one too. I just grabbed the first one I saw in my hurry."

"It was lucky," Brother Alban remarked gently. "Our trick wasn't much good, and if we'd had the right hat Felix might not have come to our aid."

"Oh, yes, I'm sure he would!" exclaimed Brother Botolph. "I'm sure he was ready, waiting with his surprises. I know our Felix. He may even have made the tricks go wrong on purpose," he ended hopefully. His failures still worried him.

"That would not have taken much magic," Brother Ubald remarked with a wry smile.

"Felix has been so wonderful to us. I'd like to give him

something in return. I'd like to give him my eggshell collection," Brother Botolph went on impetuously.

"What would he do with it?" asked Brother Ubald. "He'd rather look at it here."

"And we'd miss it," murmured Brother Alban, looking up at the mantelpiece, on which the shells were arranged in all their splendor.

"Don't worry about returning Felix's gift," said Brother

Ubald. "It makes him happy to be generous. We shall have to allow him to spoil us." He smiled to himself. "I can foresee it all—visits to the palace, an audience with the king, rides on his horse, presents—endless presents—and on a gray day, when everything is dreary, sudden magic. Ah, Felix, it was a blessed day when we took you in!"

"We almost refused him," said Brother Alban in a small, penitent voice. There was a moment's silence. Then Brother Ubald fetched his souvenir album to show the others how he'd recognized Felix's handwriting. He had kept many pages of Felix's exercises. The three dwarfs bent over the book, their gray hairs mingling as they bowed over the lamplit table, their arms on one another's shoulders. Behind them their shadows stretched across the circular wall. The grandfather clock ticked slowly. The kettle sang a glad song on the stove.

"Do you remember his first bath?" said Brother Botolph.

"And the fright we got when he started to fly?"

"Do you remember? . . . Do you remember?" The little room grew warm and sweet with young Felix's presence.

In the Squirrels' household, higher up in the tree, all was quiet. The overexcited children had at last fallen asleep, and Mamma Squirrel was picking up their clothes before going to bed herself. Her eyes were soft, like a bride's. After the party Mr. Squirrel had said to her, "Rosa, did you hear? I'm to hold myself ready. The king may want me someday." And he had looked so noble that Mamma Squirrel really could not help it. She had fallen in love with him all over again.

"Red," she called, "it's late!" There was no answer. Mamma Squirrel peered into the dressing room. There sat Mr. Squirrel, in front of the mirror, his helmet on his head and on his face a smile of ineffable and unutterable bliss.